THE CEMETERY
IN BARNES

Gabriel Josipovici was born in Nice in 1940 to Russo-Italian, Romano-Levantine parents. He lived in Egypt till 1956, when he came to Britain. He read English at St Edmund Hall, Oxford, and from 1963 to 1998 taught literature in the School of European Studies at the University of Sussex. He is the author of eighteen novels, three volumes of short stories, nine books of criticism, numerous plays for stage and radio, and a memoir of his mother, the poet and translator Sacha Rabinovitch.

THE CEMETERY IN BARNES

Gabriel
Josipovici

CARCANET

First published in Great Britain in 2018

by Carcanet Press Ltd
Alliance House, 30 Cross Street
Manchester M2 7AQ

A CIP catalogue record for this book is available from
the British Library, ISBN 9781784105464.

Book design: Luke Allan. Printed by SRP Ltd.
The publisher acknowledges financial assistance
from Arts Council England.

Supported using public funding by
ARTS COUNCIL
ENGLAND

In memory of Bernard Hoepffner
dear friend – best of translators

'I am freezing. The sky is made of iron and I of stone.'

Hölderlin to Schiller, September 1795

He had been living in Paris for many years. Longer, he used to say, than he cared to remember.

When my first wife died, he would explain, there no longer seemed to be any reason to stay in England. So he moved to Paris and earned his living by translating.

The beauty of a translator's job, he would say, is that you can do it anywhere and you don't ever need to see your employer. When a book is done you send it off and in due course you receive the remainder of your fee. Meanwhile, you have started on the next one.

He was an old-fashioned person, still put on a jacket and tie to sit down to work, and a coat and hat when he went out. Even at the height of the Parisian summer he never ventured out without his hat. At my age, he would say, it's too late to change. Besides, I'm a creature of habit, always was.

He lived in a small apartment at the top of a peeling building in the rue Lucrèce, behind the Panthéon. To get to it you went through the dark, narrow rue Saint-Julien and climbed the steep flight of steps which brought you out directly opposite the building. There were, of course, other ways of getting there, but this was the one he regularly used. It was how, in his mind, his little flat was linked to the outside world.

From his desk, if he craned, he could see the edge of the great dome of the Panthéon through the skylight. Every morning, summer and winter, he was up at six, snatched a quick look to make sure the monster was still there, shaved, dressed, made himself a light breakfast, and was sitting down to work by seven-fifteen. He kept at it till eleven, when he put on his hat and coat and descended to the world below. He stopped at the corner for a cup of coffee, did what little shopping was needed, bought a paper, then ate a sandwich with a glass of beer at a nearby café. By one-thirty he was back at his desk, where he worked till four, when he knocked off for the day.

This was the moment he looked forward to most eagerly. He kept a supply of specially imported Ceylon Orange Pekoe long-leaf tea in a little wooden box with a red dragon stamped upon it and was very precise about heating the pot, giving the leaves a chance to expand in the warmth of its belly and, once the boiling water had been poured in, about the amount of time he let it stand. After tea, in the spring and summer, he would take a stroll through the city. Sometimes this led him down to the river, at others to the Luxembourg Gardens or even as far as the Montparnasse cemetery, once known as the *Cimetière du sud*, where Baudelaire is buried. If he felt particularly well or especially adventurous he would cross the river and wander up the rue du Temple and the Jewish quarter or take a bus to Pigalle and walk down the rue des Martyrs and the Boulevard de Montmartre, through the covered passages and out into the gardens of the Palais Royal, and so to the Louvre and back to the river. Occasionally, on Sundays, he would take the underground to the flea market at the Porte de Clignancourt and walk round the strange, unreal shanty town where you could buy anything from leather jackets to art deco lampshades, from enormous kitchen tables which had stood for centuries in farmhouses in the Norman countryside to the ceremonial dresses of bygone African kings, and where he had once caught sight of Benjamin Britten and Peter Pears examining a large green limestone lingam.

He was always back by seven-thirty, in time for his reservation at a nearby bistro. He ate whatever was put in front of him and paid by the month without ever questioning the bill. After supper he would return to the flat and read a little or listen to music. He had a good collection of early music and his one indulgence was occasionally adding to it – Harnoncourt and the Concentus Musicus of Vienna he particularly admired, and he would often put on their superb recording of Monteverdi's *Orfeo* with the dazzling Jeanne Deroubaix as the Messenger:

A te ne vengo, Orfeo,
Messaggiera infelice,
Di caso più infelice e più funesto:
La tua bella Euridice…

I come to you, Orpheus,
An ill-fated bearer of tidings
Still more ill-fated and more tragic:
Your lovely Eurydice…

Sometimes you also went to concerts, his wife – his second wife – would interrupt him. And he seemed to need these interruptions, was adept at incorporating them into his discourse, using them as stepping-stones to the development of his theme.

I did, he would go on, but not often; concerts were expensive and, besides, after London, live music in Paris was nearly always a disappointment.

We listen a lot here too, his wife would say, pointing to an array of LPs on the shelves. Friends who were spending the weekend with them, and neighbours who occasionally dropped in on them in their converted farmhouse in the Black Mountains, high up above Abergavenny, were entertained to an evening of Baroque music on their excellent hi-fi equipment. His wife, a handsome woman with a mass of red hair piled up high on her head, would hand the records to him reverently, dusting them with a special cloth as she did so, but leaving the final gestures – the laying of the record on the turntable, the setting of the mechanism in motion, the gentle lowering of the stylus, the closing of the lid – to him.

I'm so uneducated, she would say. When I met him I thought a saraband was something you wore round your waist.

You had other qualities, he would say, smiling.

But an appreciation of classical music was not one of them, she would say.

Between records he would often talk about his Paris years. After the death of his first wife what he needed most was solitude, he said. Not that he wanted to brood on what had happened, he just wanted to be alone. I suppose I took on more work than was strictly necessary, he would say, but I think I needed to feel that when one book was finished there was always another waiting for me, and then another.

Sometimes, in the early morning in spring and summer, when the light was exceedingly gentle as it touched the rounded belly of the glazed earthenware teapot, he would be filled with a sense of extraordinary peace and well-being.

I would never have known moments like those if I hadn't been alone, he would say. And, in the end, you know, it's those moments that one cherishes and remembers.

As he strolled through the city in the late afternoons, his day's work done, he would occasionally have fantasies of drowning, a vivid sense of startled faces on the bank or bridge above him, or perhaps on the deck of a passing boat, and then the waters would close over him and he would sink gently down, gradually shedding a knuckle perhaps, or a tightly curled up soul, lying on the sandy bottom, rocking peaceably with the current.

He knew such feelings were neurotic, dangerous even, but he was not unduly worried, sensing that it was better to indulge them than to try and eliminate them altogether. After all, everyone has fantasies. In the one life there are many lives. Alternative lives. Some are lived and others imagined. That is the absurdity of biographies, he would say, of novels. They never take account of the alternative lives casting their shadows over us as we move slowly, as though in a dream, from birth to maturity to death.

In their converted farmhouse in the Black Mountains, high up above Abergavenny, his wife – his second wife – would serve chilled white wine to friends and neighbours who dropped in to see them, making sure no glass stayed empty for long.

You thought of alternative lives as you climbed the steps up from the rue Saint Julien, she would say. You thought of them as you descended.

Steps are conducive to fantasy, he would say. Going up and down lets the mind float free. How often we run up and down the steps of our own lives, he would say. As we run up and down the scales of a piano.

And always with his hat on, his wife would say.

Yes, always with my hat on.

You see, he would say, I'm a creature of habit. I belong to an older generation. I would have felt naked without my hat and tie.

He had to explain to me that a Baroque suite was not something elaborate you served up at the end of a meal, she would say, laughing her full-throated laugh.

You had other qualities, he would say.

She certainly made life comfortable for him, saw to it that he had everything he wanted and was not disturbed by any of the details of daily living. He for his part looked up to her, would do nothing without her consent, wanted her to say when he was tired and ready for bed, when he was hungry and ready for a meal. All their friends commented on the sense of harmony and well-being that emanated from their home in the hills high up above Abergavenny.

In a way he had been happy alone in his tiny Paris apartment. His desk was under the skylight and as he worked he felt the sun warm the top of his head and neck. When he poured the tea into his cup in the early morning silence it sometimes seemed to him as if all of existence was concentrated into that one event. Could anyone wish for greater happiness?

And yet, he would say, standing in the middle of the big living room with a glass of chilled white wine in his hand, do we always know how we really feel?

Sometimes, he said, the tediousness and unreality of the novels he was translating were too much for him. At such times it took a monumental effort to keep going till the morning break and there were even occasions when he could not face the afternoon stint. There were moments, he would say, as I sat translating those identical cardboard novels with their identical cardboard plots, when I felt as if I was choking to death.

You worked your head off, his wife would say. No one can work the hours you did, day after day, never taking a holiday. Not with the kind of mental effort translation requires.

I would stare at the page and it just wouldn't make sense any more, he would say. What had seemed so easy and enjoyable at eight o'clock in the morning would come to seem intolerable a few short hours later.

You had a great sense of responsibility, his wife would say. What translator slaves over his work as you did? What translator punishes himself as you did?

All do, he would say. With what publishers are prepared to pay us we have no alternative.

But they have families to support. Children to feed.

That's true, he would say.

Their friends were used to these exchanges, knew that his stories of his Paris years could not be told by him alone, that he needed her interjections, which functioned more like a chorus than a genuine attempt at dialogue, for you felt that they had been repeated so often that neither of them really thought any more about what they were saying.

Don't misunderstand me, he would say. I liked the work. I liked the fact that I could do things in my own way, in my own home, in my own time. And I liked the sense of peace in the room as I sat at my desk under the skylight. I liked the ritual of sharpening the pencils before I started and then sweeping the shavings into the wastepaper basket, of tapping the pile of already translated sheets until the edges were smooth and clean. I liked drawing up my chair to the desk so that my legs fitted underneath, just so. I liked adjusting the lamp until it shone down on the book at which I was working and on the fresh white sheet I had pulled towards me and left the rest of the room in semi-darkness. I liked the moment when I turned my gaze upon the last sentence and found the words already there, fully formed, as I brought the pencil down on the fresh sheet.

It was only when the meaning of what he was translating began to seep through to him, he said, that he found it difficult to go on. As long as each sentence could be seen in isolation, as a specific challenge, a unique problem, the task was not only tolerable, it was positively pleasurable. The trouble started when he began, against his will, to focus on the style and subject-matter of the novel before him.

The same characters, he would say. The same plots. Never seen in life but recurring in novel after novel, no matter if the author was an old man or a young woman, successful or unknown, as though for everyone who picked up a pen or sat down at a typewriter life had been reduced to six characters and five plots, its infinite variety, of which the authors were no doubt perfectly aware in daily life, reduced to this, as he or she sat down at the fateful desk. At those times he would find his body rebelling against the task upon which he was engaged, as though it could not or would not be a party to it. He would have difficulty breathing and would need to get up at shorter and shorter intervals to walk about the room, splash water on his face or gaze up through the skylight at the Parisian sky.

Sometimes, on bad days, when four hours at his desk were as much as he could take, he would wander without any sense of direction or purpose across the river and into the Eastern and Northern quarters of the city. Sometimes his feet would lead him to the northern cemetery of Père Lachaise, whose extraordinary funerary monuments, some resembling nothing so much as stone sentry boxes, and others like art nouveau fantasies, but all designed to testify to the wealth and respectability of the deceased and his or her family, never failed to soothe him. He would saunter down the long avenues and turn off into the side-alleys as the fancy took him, feeling strangely at home in this civilised necropolis. Afterwards, if it was cold, he would break his strict habits and go into a nearby bar to have a shot of whisky or a cup of hot chocolate.

At other times he would only go as far as the Luxembourg Gardens, where he would find a quiet spot and stretch out on a bench under the trees and close his eyes. At times he would fall asleep like that, but some residue of guilt or a sense of his vulnerability would wake him with a start and he would sit up quickly, momentarily disorientated, his heart pounding. Was

17

he on Putney Heath on a Sunday afternoon or potholing with a school party in the limestone caves of central Wales? Or had he lain down on the shingle beach in Littlehampton on a summer's day?

A man in a checked suit, middle-aged, grubby, eating a sandwich from a paper bag, observed him on one such occasion from a nearby bench as he woke up and opined that it was dangerous to fall asleep in the open air. The sun did funny things to one, he said. It wasn't as far away as one might think. Give it half a chance and it'll get you. And once it gets you, the man said, screwing his right hand up into a fist and staring down at it, it will never let you go. Never.

He did indeed feel that day as if the sun had done something brutal to him as he slept. His hat had fallen into the dust beneath the bench and his face felt red and itchy. His heart beat in his chest under his heavy clothes with an abnormal violence and there was a strange feeling in his stomach, as though it was at once empty and bloated. But after he had washed his face at a nearby fountain, combed his hair and set his hat back on, he felt almost normal. He turned to look at the man who had spoken to him but though he was still sitting there, staring at him and bringing the sandwich regularly and mechanically to his mouth, biting and chewing, he gave no sign of recognition, did not by so much as a nod of the head acknowledge that he had addressed him a little earlier.

Such days, though, were rare. Most of the time he stuck to his routine without a thought: rise, shave, dress, Panthéon, breakfast, work, steps, coffee, shopping, lunch, steps, work, tea, steps, supper, steps, music, Panthéon, bath, bed. He had always been a creature of habit, he said, and the years in Putney with his first wife – a quiet, gentle, methodical girl (they were both of them hardly more than children) – had reinforced his predilection for a simple and orderly existence.

He taught me the value of order, his wife – his second wife – would say. Before I met him I was all over the place. I didn't know if I was coming or going.

You had other qualities, he would say.

But order was not among them. No way. Order was not among them.

She had the trace of an accent, more pronounced on some days than on others, and her habit of using colloquialisms that were vaguely inappropriate or had long gone out of fashion suggested that she did not have a native speaker's instinctive grasp of register. But who could fail to be moved by her statuesque presence, her long flowing robes and her fine red hair piled with such careless ease on her noble head?

Sometimes a few of those who had come for drinks would be invited to stay for a simple lunch. While they sat looking out of the big plate-glass window, talking in low tones, he would lay the table and she would make the last adjustments to the meal before they all sat down at the fine oak dining table, one of the features of the room.

Friends who had known him in the old days would comment on the uncanny resemblance between his two wives.

He had simply wanted a change, he said, and the chance to let time do its healing work. That was why he had moved to Paris. And he recalled with pleasure the sensation of waking up in his attic room so close to the Panthéon, with its sloping ceiling and the skylight beneath which he had set up his desk.

It takes solitude to make you discover the world, he would say, kneeling by the turntable in the big living room with its splendid views over the Brecon Beacons, and lowering the stylus onto the record:

Io la Musica son, ch' ai dolci accenti
So far tranquillo ogni turbato core,
Et or nobil ira et or d'amore
Poss'infiammar le più gelate menti.

I am Music, whose sweet tones
Can soothe each troubled heart
And can with noble ire or with love
Inflame the coldest mind.

The farmhouse had been built in the eighteenth century, but like all such houses its traditional style made it difficult to date with accuracy. Its previous occupants had modernised it and installed the plate-glass window which now took up almost the whole of one wall of the living room and looked out over the valley to the mountains beyond. It was not unusual for them to have ten or fifteen people in for drinks on a Sunday morning or, occasionally, on a Saturday evening – local solicitors and schoolteachers, retired civil servants, London barristers and Oxford dons with holiday cottages in the vicinity. In the summer the curtains were never drawn and they would watch together as the last rays of the sun slowly withdrew from the peaceful valley.

The first hour of work, he would say, between seven and eight-fifteen, always gave him the greatest pleasure. Even the most convoluted sentences fell effortlessly into English forms and rhythms, and he would be conscious not so much of the meaning of the words he was translating as of himself as a kind of smoothly functioning machine, rejoicing quietly in his own ability to find the optimum solution to the problems raised by the inevitable lack of synchronicity between any two languages and cultures.

The only periods of anxiety, he recalled, came when he found himself within sight of the end of one book without the contract for the next one finalised. But he was so good at his job, worked so fast and to such good effect, that this rarely occurred. Usually, by the time he was done and ready to send off the type-script, the fruit of his labour of the previous months, another book was already lying on his desk, shiny and new, ready to be opened at the first page.

He made no plans, was happy to take each day as it came. There are times in life, he would say, when it's an achievement to get through the day.

And the steps helped. Climbing out of the rue Saint-Julien, descending from the rue Lucrèce. That was why he always made a point of leaving and returning to the flat in the same manner. Sixty-seven steps, he would say. He had got to know them well, could, after a while, have gone up or down them blindfold. As he reached the top he could feel his little studio flat bending down to meet him, could already see himself putting away his few groceries, filling the kettle, watching as it came to the boil, or listening to Monteverdi as he lolled in his bath – a surprising luxury in the Paris of those years and one of the reasons he had been so eager to take the flat.

Io la Musica son, ch'ai dolce accenti
So far tranquillo ogni turbato core.

The bathroom had no window and the ventilator did not work. The ancient bath with its clawed feet took up most of the space. All very different from the bathroom of the flat in Putney, with its boxed bath and large window looking out over the long narrow garden, where he had lived with his first wife, a trainee solicitor and amateur violinist. When he lowered himself slowly into the hot water before going to bed and the steam billowed back from the low ceiling, he felt remarkably peaceful. It was more than the simple satisfaction of having made it through another day. It was something positive, an indefinable element that made his heart stir. Lying back in the soapy water, with the strains of *Orfeo* coming through the half-open door –

Et or di nobil ira et or d'amore
Poss'infiamar le più gelate menti –

he would close his eyes and drift off, not exactly to sleep, but certainly into a state very different from that of every day.

In Putney he had often walked to the Underground station to wait for his wife as she came home from work. If the weather was fine they would meet at Putney Bridge Station and then walk back, hand in hand, across the footbridge, down into Deodar Road, and then, after a detour through the small and friendly Wandsworth Park, more continental than English with its neat lawns and great avenue of plane trees parallel to the river, up Oxford Street, across the Upper Richmond Road and so to Carlton Drive. Sometimes, as they crossed the footbridge, ducks would be flying overhead in arrow formation, squawking loudly, and once they had been fortunate enough to be on the bridge as nine swans, their wings beating the air with the sound of thunder, raced past so low overhead that he felt he had only to reach out a hand to touch their trailing feet.

The sound they made has never left me, he would say. I can hear it to this day.

Nature has always moved him, his wife – his second wife – would say.

This is the only world we have, he would say. We need to recognise how extraordinary it is.

You see what I mean, his wife would say.

The living room of the converted farmhouse in Wales which they had recently bought faced south over a broad valley, and on summer evenings the sun would slant across the room and the visitors would crowd round the plate-glass window and exclaim over the view.

It's not our doing, his wife – his second wife – would say. The people we bought it from did most of the alterations. Actually, she would say, it's completely spoiled the symmetry of the façade. These old houses were never meant to have windows this size. I sometimes wonder, she would say, whether we should replace it with something closer to the original.

However, everyone always assured her that the window was

a wonderful improvement, that if there was a view to be seen it was only right to allow it to be seen.

Oh, I like it all right, she would say. I think it's simply fabulous, actually. But he feels it destroys the character of the house. That's what comes of having a husband with taste. I've never had taste, she would say. It would be funny if I started having it now.

You had other qualities, he would say, smiling.

They never called each other by name. For her he was always *he* and for him she was always *she*. Friends of theirs wondered if they used the same formula when they were alone, but no one really knew them well enough to ask.

The flat in Putney where he lived with his first wife gave onto a long, thin garden at the end of which ran the Underground line, no longer 'under', of course, by this time. From the garden one could look up to the East Putney station platform and on rainy days he would walk round to the entrance and wait for her. Sometimes they would arrange to meet at the Queen Elizabeth Hall or at St John's, Smith Square, where they would have a bite to eat in the crypt café before attending a concert.

The revival of early music, he would say as he stood in the middle of the big living room in the Black Mountains above Abergavenny which he and his wife – his second wife – had recently bought, should not be seen as a merely antiquarian gesture. It stems from a profound revolution in our understanding of the nature of Western music. Beethoven's Ninth Symphony is no longer the ideal to which all music must aspire, as it was for many composers and concert-goers in the nineteenth century and still is for the public at large. In fact, he would say, the Ninth Symphony is recognised by all true music-lovers as something of an aberration, the culmination of a trend which, seen from our perspective in the second half of the twentieth century, looks more and more like a *cul de sac*.

Few could follow him when he began to speak in this vein, but all felt somehow pleased and flattered to be addressed in such a way. And it would, they knew, inevitably draw a riposte from her.

She did not disappoint. The only classical music I knew before I met him, she said, was hits from *Carmen* and *La Bohème*. He taught me to appreciate the Baroque and the Renaissance.

You had other qualities, he would say.

Perhaps I did, she would respond, but an appreciation of classical music was not one of them.

Friends who had known him in the old days often commented on the uncanny similarity between his two wives, all the more remarkable because, apart from the hair, they did not physically resemble each other at all.

Not many of their neighbours or acquaintances shared his passion for early music. All, however, were ready to listen. Because his wife – his second wife – knew how to make them comfortable and welcome, it was a pleasure to sit there in the old converted farmhouse in the mountains, sipping good wine and looking out over the rolling hills and valleys spreading out below them. Most of the time he talked about his life in Paris.

Paris too, he said, was changing. Soon the old village atmosphere would be gone and it would only be another splendid capital, a magnet for tourists and a playground for the rich and childless. Mind you, he would say, people have been saying that about Paris for over a century and Paris is still a delight, an anomaly among the major cities of the world. They said so when Haussmann tore down huge swathes of the right bank to drive his giant boulevards through it, down which troops would be able to march at the double and quell any new Commune, and they said it again after France began to relinquish its colonies, when the influx of Vietnamese and Algerians seemed to threaten forever its uniquely French character. And they will go on saying it for a long time to come. But Paris will survive.

It was not, however, only the quaint old Paris whose streets he walked during those solitary years after the death of his first wife. Sometimes he took a bus to the poverty-stricken Northern or Eastern suburbs, or found solace traipsing through the anonymous streets round the Porte d'Italie and the Porte d'Orleans. What you need at certain periods in life, he would say, is simply the feeling that things are going on all around you, that people are busy with their lives, that there is a world out there which exists and of which you will never know anything. I don't know why, he would say, but such knowledge is a great balm for the troubled spirit.

If, for some reason – rain, cold, sheer laziness – he did not take his afternoon walk, he found it difficult to sleep at night. Fragments of *Orfeo* would float into his head, or verses from the *Regrets* of du Bellay, which he had picked up second-hand in one of the little stalls that line the *quais* and which, in his more ambitious moments, he had even tried translating for his own amusement:

La Muse ainsi me fait sur ce rivage,
Où je languis banny de ma maison,
Passer l'ennuy de la triste saison
Seule compagne à mon si long voyage.

Or:

On dit qu'Achille en remaschant son ire
De tels plaisirs souloit s'entretenir
Pour addoulcir le triste souvenir
De sa maistresse, aux fredons de sa lyre.

Or:

De quelque mal un chacun se lamente,
Mais les moyens de plaindre son divers:
J'ay, quant a moy, choisi celuy des vers
Pour desaigrir l'ennuy qui me tormente.

Though he was tempted to get out of bed and sit down at his desk to try and see if such lines would go into English pentameters ('Thus does the Muse upon this alien shore / Where I am stuck, an exile from my home…'?), he resisted the temptation and kept his eyes shut tight, trying to count sheep jumping over fences or even the specific lambs he and his wife – his first wife – had once seen in a sloping field, running and butting each other in sheer high spirits, as they were on their way back by train from a brief holiday in Snowdonia. But the lines would not let him go ('They say Achilles, chewing on his ire, / Would strive to take his pleasure in such toys, / Sweetening the memory of the joys / His girl provided, by playing on his lyre.'?)

She finished work at five and he knew that if he set off from the house at a quarter past he would not have long to wait at Putney Bridge Station. That was when the days were fine and she did not go directly from her office in Holborn to a friend's house to rehearse. She had been an excellent amateur violinist and it was a great sadness to her that he could not play with her. But he had never had a chance to learn an instrument and she assured him she would not have him other than he was.

Sometimes he started a little earlier and stopped at the public library in Disraeli Road to change a book, or he made a detour via the Upper Richmond Road to see what was showing at the local fleapit, and if the film was of interest he would drop in to see it the following afternoon. They would not speak or even kiss, just hold hands and stroll back over the footbridge; and sometimes, as they walked, she would shut her eyes and let him lead her.

He felt at times as if he did not understand her at all. She was there and yet she was not there. He held her and yet he did not hold her. As they walked, hand in hand, he sometimes felt as if he was walking with a stranger.

To supplement the meagre income his translation brought him he tried giving English lessons. Someone at his wife's office gave her the phone number of a family looking for a tutor for their daughter. They were wealthy Greeks, shipping millionaires, who lived in Harley Street. A servant brought in coffee and baklava and the mother explained what he would have to do. My Lula is a highly intelligent girl, she said. We want her to go to university. But she finds studying difficult. It's understandable at her age. I was just the same. I want someone to stimulate her interest in English literature.

He said he would do his best and sized up Lula, a languid flower reclining on the sofa next to her mother. She gazed back at him without interest.

Emily Dickinson was on the A-level syllabus, so he thought, when he came round a week later to take up his duties, that they might start there.

Let's have a look at 'A narrow fellow in the grass', he said.

He waited but the girl did not react. She sat opposite him at the table, head bowed.

Have you got the book? he asked.

Yes, she said.

Where is it?

Upstairs.

I asked you to have it to hand.

With a sigh she got up, left the room and returned a few minutes later with the book.

She sat down opposite him with another sigh.

Go on, he said. Open it.

With what seemed like a huge effort she opened the book.

Have you got it?

She shook her head.

Look at the back, he said. Find it in the index of first lines.

He waited, his own copy open in front of him.

Well? he said. Found it?

Yes.

Read it then.

She stared down at the book.

Out loud, he said.

29

He waited.

Go on, he said.

No, she said after a while. You read it. I can't.

Yes you can. Go on.

He waited.

Finally he said: All right. I will.

He pulled the book to him and read:

A narrow fellow in the grass
Occasionally rides –
You may have met Him – did you not
His notice sudden is.

What, he asked, is the narrow fellow?

She sat staring down at her book.

Well, he said. Go on.

I don't know.

Have a guess.

He waited.

A narrow fellow in the grass? he prompted.

She turned her soulful eyes on him.

What is narrow?

Like this.

And fellow?

A man.

OK. A male something, like this, in the grass.

She was silent, eyes down.

Lula, he said. We're not going to get very far if you go on like this.

She did not move.

Lula, he said.

She raised her head and looked at him.

Well? he said.

It bores me, she said.

Do you want to pass your exams?

She shrugged her shoulders.

What do you want to do with your life?

I don't know.

Then there's not much I can do for you, is there?

She turned her great eyes on him once again.

OK, he said. That will be all for today.

All?

Yes.

In the salon the mother waited for him.

Well? she said.

I can't do it, he said. She has no wish to learn.

But she must go to university.

He shrugged.

You know what girls are like at her age, she said.

He waited.

Very well, she said. How much do I owe you?

His next pupil was the small and fiery daughter of a banker in Hampstead.

Where did you study? she asked him.

Oxford, he said.

Which college?

He told her.

Did you like it?

It was all right.

I'm going to Cambridge. They make you think in Cambridge, in Oxford they only make you read books.

Who told you that?

My English teacher.

And how does he know?

He went to Cambridge.

But not to Oxford.

He's an excellent teacher. I trust his judgement.

I don't quite understand why your father hired me, he said. You seem to know exactly what you want to do and to be perfectly able to do it by yourself.

He is convinced that the more money he spends on my education the better the results.

And you don't agree with him.

I'm a Marxist.

What does that mean?

You want me to explain?

I thought I was supposed to help you with your English? he said.

Everything's connected, she said.

Then I suppose you'd better.

It was only in Paris, he said, that he began to listen to music properly. Of course he had once lived with a musician and even been to concerts with her. But he was not encouraged to listen to her and her friends practising since, as she pointed out, quartet playing is something done among friends and for its own sake, and the whole atmosphere would be altered if someone not actually involved in making music were to sit there listening without taking part. Thus the kind of concentrated attention he now began to give to music, evening after evening, sitting with his eyes closed in the rocking chair, was for him something entirely new:

Tu se'morta, mia vita, ed io respiro?
Tu se' da me partita
Per mai più not tornare, ed io rimango?
No...

You are dead, my life, and I breathe on?
You have left me
Never to return, while I remain?
No...

It was a mystery how the simple flowing lines of Monteverdi could have such an effect on one, filling one with a strange emotion which seemed to consist of both joy and sorrow, both bitterness and a sweetness past imagining:

N'andrò sicuro a'più profondi abissi,
E intenerito il cor del Re dell'ombre,
Meco trarrotti a riveder le stele,
Oh, se ciò negherammi empio destino,
Rimarrò teco, in compagnia di morte
Addio terra, addio cielo e sole, addio.

I shall go down to the most profound abyss,
And, having softened the heart of the King of Shades,
Bring you back with me to see the stars again;
Or, if an evil fate denies me this,
With you I will remain in the company of the dead.
Farewell earth! Farewell sky and sun, farewell!

He would take his time over dinner, reading the paper or studying his fellow diners, then climb the steps to the little flat and spend the evening reading or listening to Monteverdi, first sitting in the rocking chair in the corner and then lying in the bath with the door open and steam billowing up to the ceiling and down again, for the fan had long since ceased to function and the landlord was elusive.

You are dead, oh my life, and I breathe on?
You have left me
Never to return, and I remain?
No...

He loved to lie in the large, old-fashioned tub with his feet flat against the tap end, two purple blobs barely visible through the steam. He thought of those large paintings Bonnard had done of his wife Marthe lying in her bath, where the bathroom tiles are so alive and the floating woman so like a corpse. Why did they move him so much, while that huge painting by one of the pre-Raphaelites – Millais, was it? or Burne-Jones? – of the drowned Ophelia, said to be the most popular picture in the Tate, left him totally unmoved? Was it because the pre-Raphaelite artist had put all his effort into making Ophelia pathetic while Bonnard had put his into catching the light of the bathroom, forcing us to recognise that we are all temporal creatures, emerging into the light for a few brief seconds before we disappear again?

As often as not, while he was caught up in these imponderables the record would come to an end, jerking him back into the present. He would leap up, grab a towel, dry his feet as best he could on the mat, and dash into the room to turn it over, then, back in the bathroom, slowly dry himself and put on his pyjamas.

On weekends in Putney he and his wife would often cycle along the towpath to Kew or Richmond Park and, in Kew, go and see the exotic plants in one of the greenhouses or, in Richmond Park, wander through the ferns looking out for the deer. In Paris the days merged into one another and he saw no reason, his job being what it was, ever to take a day off from his strict routine.

You were always so conscientious, his wife – his second wife – would say. You would sooner have died than been late with a typescript.

If I hadn't had my routine I don't know what would have happened to me, he would say. It was the routine that kept me going.

You have to draw the line between a fruitful and a compulsive routine, she would say. The trouble is he could never draw that line.

But can one always know where the line is to be drawn? he would ask, smiling.

All their friends agreed that there was a remarkable sense of peace pervading their house. You could feel it, they would say, the moment you stepped inside the front door.

Peace comes with happiness, he would say, and who can say where happiness comes from?

Sometimes, on a Sunday, after a morning in Richmond Park, they would sit in a pub by the river and have lunch. His wife didn't talk much, did not pester him with questions about his work. She sat with her eyes closed and a smile on her lips, her face turned to the sun which glinted in her corn-blond hair and brought out the touches of red in it. Afterwards they would retrieve their bicycles and ride home along the towpath.

As he sat in his armchair, high up above the rue Lucrèce, listening to his latest purchase, he would allow his mind to wander back to his years in Putney. Sometimes hours would go by in this fashion and he would suddenly wake up to the fact that the record had come to an end and was still turning round and round with a faint hiss. He would stare into space for a few minutes, willing himself to get up and turn it over, though often he would merely lurch forward and pull the plug out before settling back again in the armchair and closing his eyes. Gradually the hum of traffic from the rue Saint Jacques would rise up and assail his ears, but he would not move.

One day, indulging his drowning fantasies more than usual, he did not go back to his room after lunch. Instead he walked down the hill and across the river to the Île Saint-Louis and then across again and up in the direction of the Bastille. He must have walked for two or three hours, his mind a blank, because he suddenly realised that he felt utterly exhausted and could not walk another step. There was a café on the other side of the road, so he crossed over and went in. It was empty at that time of day except for the *patron* in his shirtsleeves, polishing the counter. He eased himself onto a stool and ordered a coffee. When it came he downed it in one go and ordered another. The acrid taste sent a shudder through him.

When the second cup arrived he toyed with it a little longer, dipping a lump of sugar and watching the dark liquid eat into the white cube, letting the brown fragments drop into the coffee as he slowly stirred, gazing down at the spoon as he did so. By the time he had drunk his second cup he felt restored and wondered how he could have reached the state of exhaustion he had just been in.

I need to make a call, he said to the *patron*, who was busy at the other end of the counter.

The man stood in front of him, separated by the wide expanse of polished chrome. He was a large man with a red face, his head bald and shiny as a billiard ball but, as if to make up for it, with a bristling moustache and large amounts of black hair sprouting from his ears and covering his arms.

A token, please, he repeated. For a phone call.

He thought the man had not heard, then saw that he was in fact holding out his hand, palm upwards. The silver token lay there on his pink skin.

He looked into the man's face again. He was grinning, revealing a mouth full of gleaming white teeth and holding out his hand across the polished counter. There it lay, waiting to be picked up. Gingerly he moved his hand forward and reached for it, but just as he was about to pick it up he realised it was no longer there. The large hand was open, palm upwards, but it was empty.

He looked up quickly. The man was still grinning, staring mockingly back at him. He lowered his eyes again and as he did so the man slowly turned his hand over and there was the token again, a small silver circle lying on the hairy back of the hand. The man thrust his arm forward across the counter, as if to say: Go on, take it. So, once again, he watched his own hand going out to meet the other, and this time his fingers closed round the token and he lifted it off the hand and drew it back towards him. As he did so he saw the hole. It was a small round black hole in the middle of the man's hand, just where the token had been, and it was smoking gently.

He must have walked a lot more after that. He didn't remember where or for how long, but towards the end of the afternoon he found himself by the river again. Automatically he began to browse the bookstalls on the *quais* but his mind wouldn't focus. He didn't want to go back to his flat but his feet felt swollen and were hurting and he felt he had to take off his shoes or he would begin to cry. He found some stairs and staggered down them to the level of the water. There was a patch of grass at the bottom where a tree grew under a high wall. He sat down slowly, leaning back against the trunk, closed his eyes and fumbled with the laces of his shoes. When his feet were free at last he opened his eyes again and sat motionless, staring down at the water.

When the girl came it had grown almost dark. He couldn't make out her face, only the glint of red hair under a little green beret. For a moment, in the half-light, she reminded him of his wife.

He must have spoken, because she said: You are English?

Yes.

I guess.

Oh?

Yes. I guess.

He couldn't place her accent.

It is hot today, she said.

Yes.

He wanted to talk to her about the token but checked himself.

She took off the beret, shaking her head and releasing a mass of red hair, which fell in cascades round her shoulders.

Hold please, she said, handing him the beret. It was curiously small and soft.

She had taken a brush out of her little bag and was brushing her hair, moving her head in time to the strokes. Then the brush vanished as abruptly as it had appeared and she took the beret back from him, swept up her hair and put it on again, this time at rather more of an angle than before.

He was looking at the lights of the city reflected in the water when she said to him: Can I put my head here, yes?

Without waiting for a reply she swung round, tucking her legs under her skirt, and laid her head on his lap.

Her eyes were closed and he thought she had gone to sleep, but then she began to move her head on his lap, slowly at first, as though trying to find the most comfortable position, then with gathering violence. He stroked her hair. The beret fell off, releasing her hair once again. She began to moan.

They must have got up together. He could remember nothing after that except that her room was red. Like fire, she said.

He found himself walking again, swaying like a drunk in the noonday blaze of a Parisian summer. His trousers felt too tight, his thighs itched where the cloth rubbed against the skin. His whole body felt as though it had been scraped with a knife from his forehead to the soles of his feet.

When he finally stumbled home he was so tired he could hardly get the key into the lock. He fell onto the bed fully clothed and was immediately asleep.

When he woke it was dark. He didn't know if he had slept for six hours or sixty. To judge from his ravening hunger it was probably the latter. He found some food in the fridge and wolfed it down. Then he struggled into his pyjamas and crawled into bed.

The next time he awoke it was early morning. He groped his way out of bed and to the window for his daily look at the dome of the Panthéon. As he was doing so, craning a little to the left as usual, he remembered that all had not been entirely normal in the past day or two. Alternative lives, he thought to himself, then made his breakfast and settled down to translating the novel on his desk.

It was only that evening, as he was having his bath, that he saw the wound. It was a long, straight cut, like the scratch of a cat, and ran all the way from the top of his right thigh to the knee. He touched it gently but it didn't hurt. He dried it carefully, examined it again and decided that there was nothing to do but to let it heal and disappear. In fact, though, it never entirely disappeared. Years later, in Wales, whenever he talked of his Paris years he would point to his leg and laugh and say: It never healed.

You didn't want it to, his wife would say.

Friends who had known him in the old days would comment on the resemblance between his two wives. Especially when his second wife stood in the middle of the room like that, dusting an LP before handing it to him saying, You really didn't want it to, did you?

No, he would say, looking at her as he crouched by the turntable, waiting to receive the disk from her. No I didn't, did I?

He's so superstitious, she would say. He never went to a doctor about it.

What could a doctor do?

Maybe give you something to get rid of it.

We've all got something like that somewhere on our bodies, he would say. Maybe if we got rid of it we wouldn't be ourselves any more. Who knows?

He would tell of his fantasies of drowning, vivid images he experienced at the time he was living in Paris after the death of his first wife. As I sank I would feel quite relieved, he would say. I would think: There goes another life – and know I had not finished with this one.

One sprouts so many selves, he would say, and look at her and smile. One is a murderer. One a suicide. One lives in Paris. One in Bombay. One in New York.

One, one, one, she would echo, mocking him.

Occasionally, in Putney, he would wait outside Putney Bridge tube station, but not in his usual place. Hidden behind a newspaper stand he would observe the commuters streaming

41

out of the station, heads bowed, eyes blank with weariness. Then he would see her. She would stand for a moment at the exit, not looking round for him but simply waiting for him to come up to her if he was there. After a few seconds, when he did not appear, she would start off across the street and disappear under the shadow of the footbridge.

I remember her so clearly, he would say, as she stood quite still, waiting, and the crowds swirled round her. I remember her so well.

He would give her time to climb the stairs, then slowly follow. It moved him to see her like this, from the outside, as it were, a young woman with a light step and straight fair-to-reddish hair. She never turned round or stopped to look at the water but continued on her way, evenly, unhurriedly. And he, walking always a good way behind, did not take his eyes off her.

As she turned into Carlton Drive he would walk on down the Upper Richmond Road towards Wandsworth, then circle back over the little footbridge above the girls' school, giving her time to get home and settle before he himself returned. He never told her he had been following her. When driven, as he often was, by her lack of curiosity about the way he had spent his day to give her a detailed account of his comings and goings, he always made sure he left the last hour or two vague.

Though he loved words and the rhythms of language he had neither the desire nor the ability to make something of his own with them. What made him happy, he realised, was the act of sitting down at his desk, the feel of the stack of empty sheets of foolscap under his hand and the lamp shining on the open book in front of him. Occasionally he felt a tug at his heart at the thought of how utterly useless and without consequence the work was that he was doing, but when this did happen he would quickly remind himself how lucky he was to be able to earn his living in his own way, without the need to travel to and from a place of work, or have to take orders from people he could not stand. And though at first he had to suffer the indignity of being a private tutor in order to supplement his meagre translator's income, by the time he got to Paris his stock had so risen with the publishers for whom he worked that he was able to live, if only just, on what he earned from his translations. I am one of the lucky ones, he would say to the friends who were visiting Paris and with whom he would have a meal or a drink. My needs are simple. I do what I am good at and the world is prepared to leave me alone. What more could I want?

It was in Paris that he had begun to translate the sonnets of du Bellay. He worked at mealtimes, or while waiting for the bus, or – sometimes – in the evening, with *Orfeo* or the *Goldberg Variations* (he preferred the harpsichord of Gustav Leonhard to the overhyped piano-playing of Glenn Gould) on the gramophone.

Je ne chante (Magny), je pleure mes ennuys;
   Ou, pour le dire mieulx, en pleurant je les chante,
   Si bien qu'en les chantant, souvent je les enchante:
   Voyla pourquoy (Magny) je chante jours et nuicts.

How wonderful to be able to use a friend's name in that way in a poem, he thought, and what is a translator to do with that marvellous mute 'l' in *mieulx* and 'c' in *nuicts*, which slows down the reading and gives the word a definition and a weight which the modern French *mieux* and *nuit* simply do not have? Or is this only our perception? Would a sixteenth-century Frenchman not perhaps have felt exactly the same about *mieulx* with an 'l' as his modern French counterpart feels towards *mieux* without? Be that as it may, to the modern ear and eye the earlier spelling gives a weight, a strangeness, to the word which the modern spelling does not and colours how we read. But how to carry that across in English?

> I do not sing, Magny, but weep my woes,
> Or rather say, in weeping I them chant,
> So that by chanting them I them enchant:
> And that is why, Magny, I sing both day and night.

And since this is a quatrain about enchantment, the old-fashioned 'I them chant' and 'I them enchant' – so difficult to justify in a modern translation, and not even present in du Bellay's direct and workaday syntax – almost come off. Almost. Never quite. But almost, he came to recognise, was the best he at any rate could hope for.

Even then, so many years later, in the secluded farmhouse in the Black Mountains, he could still recall the volume he had used: a paperback edition of the *Antiquités de Rome* and the *Regrets*, with the reproduction of a painting of the ruins of Rome by some Renaissance artist on the cover.

He gave me a copy of that book when we first met, his wife – his second wife – would say. He even wrote a charming dedication on the inside.

44

I loved it as though I had written it myself, he would say. And now I doubt if there is even a copy of it in the house.

Everything has its time, she would say. When its time has passed it is foolish to lament it.

He agreed with her, admired her sturdy common sense, her handsome bearing, her way with people. Their friends and acquaintances commented on the harmony of their relationship and on the peace and calm that was so palpable the moment one entered their house.

Not that life in Paris had lacked peace and calm. If your habits are regular, he would say as he selected another record to put on the gramophone, then you are in a position to respond to the world and its gifts. But most of us, most of the time, spurn these gifts and complain about our lot.

He had never been the complaining type, he said, had always accepted even the most painful blows with a kind of stubborn resignation.

Stubborn makes it sound so good, his wife – his second wife – would say, but in reality, if you want to know my opinion, it's not so different from being one of the living dead.

The line is thin, he would admit, but it is still there.

In your head, she would say.

That's where it should be, he would say.

To tell the truth, she would say, he did not much like living alone.

I did and I didn't, he would say.

You didn't but you tried to pretend that you did.

There was no pretence about it, he would say. I did and I didn't.

45

You see, his wife would say. Stubborn.

There are joys in solitude which one can never experience in married life.

Perhaps, she would say. But marriage saved you from despair.

Who's the stubborn one? he would ask as he handed her the record he had chosen, while busying himself with the gramophone.

I'm not stubborn, she would say. I'm right.

Sometimes their closest neighbours, a retired civil servant and his plain buck-toothed wife, would stay to lunch and help clear away the glasses and the nuts. The wife would put on a kitchen apron, invariably choosing the yellow plastic one with *See what I can do with a knife* and the appropriate image emblazoned on the front, and wash up the dirty glasses while her husband helped lay the table, exchanging *risqué* jokes *sotto voce* with the mistress of the house. Whenever they visited he would make a point of bringing a bouquet of flowers, freshly picked from his garden or greenhouse, handing it to her with a flourish.

He had first come across du Bellay in the lending library in Putney. He was acquainted from his undergraduate studies with the poetry of Wyatt and even of Ronsard, and could not re-read Shakespeare's early poems too often, especially *Venus and Adonis* with its lovely line, 'The sea hath bounds but deep desire hath none', but as soon as he opened du Bellay's poems that day in the Putney library he knew this was the poet for him.

Entre les loups cruels j'erre parmy la plaine,
Je sens venir l'hyver, de qui la froide haleine
D'une tremblante horreur fait herrisser ma peau.

Amidst the cruel wolves I wander, lost,
And feel the winter come, whose icy frost
With trembling horror makes my skin to crawl.

Poetry was his first love, his wife would say as she poured out the drinks for their guests in the sun-filled living room of their converted farmhouse high up in the Black Mountains above Abergavenny. As for me, she would say, I had never read a poem before I met him. It was he who taught me to understand poetry and to appreciate it.

You had other qualities, he would say.

Perhaps, she would say, but the appreciation of poetry was not amongst them.

Their friends were all in awe of her, but they found her laughter infectious and envied him his good fortune and the serenity of their life together.

One does not easily get over something like that, he would say, referring to the death of his first wife. It takes time to begin to live again, time to take your place in the world again.

They had been standing on the bank, close to the Harrods Depository, looking down at the water. Then a gust of wind had caught her straw hat and lifted it off her head. She must have slipped as she lunged for it, and the bank seemed to crumble beneath her feet. She cried out and was gone.

He had stood for a moment, panic-stricken, wondering what

he had done. He could see her blonde head bobbing about in the water beneath him, fighting the current, but the bank fell away steeply where he stood and, short of jumping in after her, there was nothing he could do. She was a much better swimmer than he and he was sure she would soon turn and swim downstream until she found a place where she could get out. And this, in time, she did.

They did not speak as they walked home. He held her close and he could feel her shivering uncontrollably beneath her thin summer dress. I will never forget how she shivered, he said. How uncontrollably she shivered.

In Paris the days followed each other with monotonous regularity. I have always been a creature of habit, he said. I was a creature of habit before I married and I remained one after my marriage. We do not change, he would say as his wife – his second wife – poured the drinks for their guests in the living room of their converted farmhouse in the Black Mountains. Today too I make sure I stick to my little routines.

I make sure he sticks to his little routines, his wife would say, laughing her deep-throated laugh.

Only when you do things automatically, he would say, is there a chance of being surprised. And what is life without surprises?

I loved my solitude and my routine, he would say. I loved waking up in the morning and peering out of the skylight to catch my first glimpse of the dome of the Panthéon in the greyness of a Parisian winter or the bright sunshine of a Parisian spring. I loved putting on my hat and starting down the stairs of the house and then down the steps outside. I loved buying the same things in the same shops and eating the same food in the same bars and bistros, day after day. I loved coming back to my room in the evening and listening to my records. And I loved running my bath last thing at night, then getting in and letting the stains of the day flow slowly out of me into the warm water.

Of course, he would say, there are times, with such an existence, when for no reason that you can understand, everything turns black. There are times when the order you have so carefully established seems suddenly unable to protect you from the darkness.

That's when it's time to get married, his wife – his second wife – would say.

Perhaps it is and perhaps it isn't.

No perhaps about it. No perhaps at all.

Sometimes their closest neighbours, a retired civil servant and his wife, would stay to lunch. The wife would lay the table in gloomy silence while her husband helped their hostess wash the glasses at the sink, howling with laughter at some joke she had made. He had a strange braying laugh, which rose to a pitch, was suddenly cut short, rose again, and abruptly died.

I wonder what the joke is, the wife would say, but he would not answer, standing as he usually did when he was alone by the plate-glass window, looking down into the valley below and across at the glorious mountains of Wales.

Occasionally, in Paris, he would spend his evenings struggling to render the sonnets of du Bellay into English. He had read somewhere, and he agreed with the criticism, that those of du Bellay's friend and more famous contemporary, Ronsard, could often be cut down from fourteen to ten lines without suffering unduly; du Bellay's, never.

Maintenant je pardonne à la doulce fureur,
Qui m'a faict consumer le meilleur de mon aage,
Sans tirer aultre fruict de mon ingrat ouvrage,
Que le vain passetemps d'une si longue erreur.

He loved the old spellings, *doulce, faict, aultre, fruict*, and the absolute but totally unforced regularity of the rhymes. He loved the two 'a's in *aage*, which enacts, as one sees it, and makes one feel in one's mouth as one says it, the slow passing of the years. He loved the way a word like *erreur* retained its primal sense of *errer*, to wander, just as the word *amazed*, he had learned as a student, conveyed to Spenser and Milton the sense of being lost in a maze. Ronsard had the greater ease, the greater charm, but it was precisely the lack of charm, the sense of someone striving not to please or delight but rather to set things down exactly as he felt them, which moved him so in du Bellay. It seemed to him that, hidden in these little sonnets, seemingly so perfunctory, so matter-of-fact, lay the secret of life itself, if only he could find it. But when he tried to make them his own, to render them into acceptable modern English, he lost the rhymes; and then, he began to realise, he had lost everything, for it was in the tension between the strict formality of the sonnet, its metre and rhyme, and the urgent and seemingly artless content, that their mystery lay. Yet when he tried to retain the rhymes he lost the ease and simplicity of the original. More often than not he would lay down his notebook without having achieved anything and go into the little bathroom, run the bath, and return to put away the book and take the cover off the bed and put it on the armchair before returning to the bathroom to brush his teeth, by which time the bath would be full.

Oblivious of his presence, she would walk ahead of him along the footbridge, as quietly and in as self-contained a manner as she always did when they were together. In the evenings he would question her about her day at the office and her return journey, or probe to see if she perhaps had an inkling that he had been following her, but she remained noncommittal, saying that nothing of note had happened, that everything was as it had always been, the tube as crowded and her final walk home as much of a relief as usual. He would apologise again for not having been at the station to meet her, but she would only shrug her shoulders and say it didn't matter, it was more important that he get on with his work. At times like that he wanted to scream, to shake her by the shoulders and ask her what did matter to her, but he was not that kind of person, so he merely turned away and busied himself with the dishes to hide from her an emotion which he did not fully understand himself.

Sometimes, in the early afternoons, he would wander along the towpath and find himself looking round after the loving couples who had just passed him, and sometimes after the girls walking their dogs who always seemed so carefree and yet so self-contained. He always half hoped that they too would be looking back, but when, occasionally, this happened, he was overcome by confusion and hurried on, hoping they had not noticed him.

Sometimes the quartet rehearsed in their flat in Putney, but most often at the home of some other member of the group who lived nearer the centre of town. The quartet consisted of his wife, a school friend and her solicitor husband, and a bearded maths teacher called Frederick Aspinall. He liked to hear them at work in the living room and would sometimes, on his way to the bathroom or the kitchen, stop by the door to listen. Once, as he stood there with his ear to the door, it suddenly opened and the maths teacher, coming out in a hurry, almost banged into him.

Frightfully sorry! he muttered. Didn't see you there in the gloom!

Though he had, in the course of his life, read or seen most of Shakespeare's plays, it was the early poems, the so-called erotic epyllia, that he found himself returning to again and again as he sat high above the street in his quiet Paris flat. *Venus and Adonis* in particular he could not read often enough, turning the words over in his mouth as though to suck the last ounce of sweetness from them.

She red and hot as coals of glowing fire,
He red for shame, and frosty in desire.

Or:

And nuzzling in his flank the loving swine
Sheathed unaware the tusk in his soft groin.

The first hour of the day was the best of all as, breakfast over, he sat down in the early morning light, drew the pile of white sheets towards him, made sure his pencil was well sharpened (he always wrote with an HB pencil, easy to erase), re-read the last sentence he had translated the day before, and plunged in. He always began a new day's work on a new sheet, a habit he had acquired in the course of his very first professional translation. Even the dullest, the most absurd and badly written books were, for that first hour, a pleasure to translate. He felt himself flowing forward in a curious and delightful combination of concentration and relaxation in which no problem was too difficult to solve almost instantly, and he hardly ever had recourse to a dictionary.

Towards the end of the hour, though, he would gradually start to become conscious of what he was doing. First he would become aware of the pleasure his work was affording him and the ease with which he was moving forward, and then he would find himself slowing down, chewing on his pencil a little more frequently than before, realise he was spending more and more time looking around the room than actually at work, and, finally, get up from his desk in disgust.

Concentration is a mysterious thing, he would say. Why are some people so much better at it than others? Why is one so much more alert one day than another?

To concentrate you have to be happy, his wife – his second wife – would say. If you're unhappy it's no surprise that your mind wanders.

It depends what you mean by happy, he would say.

Happy is happy, she would say. There are no two ways about it.

Once he had gone up to the house in Islington where she was playing with her friends after work. He had waited behind a tree, keeping watch on the front door, and when she had finally come out, alone, had followed her to the underground station and all the way home. He often wondered whether she had seen him that day. She had looked round once or twice and, at Earl's Court, where they had to change from the Piccadilly to the District Line, he had found himself dangerously close to her on the escalator. He had kept his head down and, outside, on the platform, had taken care to merge with the waiting crowd. He was almost certain he had got away with it but could never, in the nature of things, be sure. As ever, she gave nothing away.

It was as he was drying himself after his bath, one foot in the eddying water and the other on the edge of the bathtub, that he saw it, a long thin scar stretching from his right knee to the top of his thigh.

It never completely healed, he would say as he spoke of those Paris years. See, I still have it.

You never wanted it to heal, his wife – his second wife – would say.

How does one know what one wants? he would say, smiling as he carefully took the record from her.

Io la Musica son, ch'ai dolci accenti
So far tranquillo ogni turbato core.

He had found the little volume at the end of a shelf in the local library in Putney and taken it home, not knowing what

54

to expect. But as soon as he opened it he knew that this was the book for him. He had read it through a dozen times before he had to bring it back and he only did so after he had gone out and bought the identical book at the French Bookshop on King's Road. After that he carried it with him everywhere, when he set out on his afternoon walks along the towpath or over the Heath or in the tube as he went to meet his wife to go to a concert.

I do not sing, Magny, but weep my woes,
Or rather say that weeping I them chant,
So that by chanting them I them enchant:
And that is why, Magny, I sing both day and night.

It did not matter who Magny was, he lives in this poem almost as much as does the poet, a sympathetic friend to whom it is possible to write. *The Regrets* are full of such friends.

Do not be surprised, Ronsard, you who are half of me,
If France reads no more of your du Bellay.

Do not think, Robertet, that Rome as it is now
Is like the Rome which once so pleased you.

Mauny, let us take a liking to bad luck,
For how long does the good kind last?

You never see me, Pierre, without saying
That I should study less and make love instead.

55

By talking to his absent friends, du Bellay begins to understand who he is. Without them there would have been no *Regrets*. Without them he would have remained mute. For you never just talk to yourself. You have to have another to talk to, even when you are alone.

We are social beings, she would say. We need others in order to be ourselves.

That's true, he would say. Yet we also need solitude.

He did not literally pull up his trousers to show them the scar, but so vivid was his description that all their friends and acquaintances were sure that at some point they had seen it.

I was in my bath, he would say, scrubbing myself automatically as one does and feeling vaguely uneasy without quite being able to put my finger on the source of my unease, and then drying myself slowly and methodically as I always did, with my foot on the edge of the bath and my leg bent at the knee, when I saw it: a long thin line running from my right knee to the thigh, the kind of scar a cat leaves when it scratches you. I looked at it in astonishment. I didn't know what to do.

So you did nothing, his wife would say.

I mean I did not know how to account for it.

Perhaps you did not want to.

Perhaps.

Perhaps perhaps perhaps, she would say mockingly. Always perhaps.

He would look at her in admiration as she stood wiping the record before passing it to him, or handing round the drinks in the sun-filled room where they entertained their guests. When he laid it on the turntable and gently lowered the stylus every-one would stop talking.

Ma tu, gentil cantor, s'a tuoi lamenti
Già festi lagrimar queste campagne,
Perch'ora al suon de la famosa cetra
Non fai teco gioir le valli e i poggi?

But you, gentle singer, since your laments
Once wrung from these fields tears of sorrow,
Why now do you not, with your renowned lyre,
Make the hills and valleys ring with joy?

He could not understand why she asked that particular cou-ple to lunch and his heart sank when he found himself with the horse-faced wife who had nothing to say to him and to whom he had nothing to say. Once she cornered him by the sofa and started to complain about her husband, accusing him of cruelty, insensitivity, indifference, philandering. He tried to squirm past but she had him trapped.

Do you think I don't know what's going on in that kitchen? she said. Do you think I'm so blind I can't see what they're up to?

Up to? he said.

Don't give me that, she said.

I'm not giving you anything, he said.

She turned away from him with a strange snorting sound and he took the opportunity to move unobtrusively as far away from her as he could.

He loved to talk about those distant days in Paris when he would sit down to work at seven-fifteen every morning and by eleven o'clock feel that he had earned his morning cup of coffee. On his strolls through the city he had come to know it well, the stalls on the rue Moufetard, the smart shops on the rue de Rivoli, the cemeteries and the gardens, the alleys and the arcades. Only the museums I avoided, he said. It was as if not just my mind but my body had no desire to take in the fruits of a culture on which I had once been so keen.

Sometimes, in the early morning, in the summer, the light shone most gently on the earthenware teapot and, seeing it, he would feel tears come into his eyes. I could never have experienced that light if I had not been alone, he would say. I could never have felt as I did then that I wanted to bless the world and be blessed by it in turn.

When he got back to the little flat after lunch he would hang up his hat on the peg and sit straight down to work. He liked those long afternoon sessions with nothing to disturb him except the occasional sound of a police siren in the Boulevard Saint-Germain. He liked the sense of himself at work in his high room and Paris busily going about its business far below.

Time stands still when you are working, he would say.

Time never stands still, his wife – his second wife – would say.

For me, at the time, it did.

But it never does.

As you will.

No, she would say. Not as I will. It never does. Period.

You are right, of course, he would concede, but, since I felt it did there was a sense in which it did.

He can't get rid of me that easily, she would say, laughing her full-throated laugh. He thinks he can but he can't.

It's not a question of getting rid, he would say, it's a question of perception.

And you perceived time standing still?

Sometimes.

Sometimes, sometimes, she would mock him.

It was like a repetition of their marriage vows, and the guests were sometimes tempted to clap at a particularly pithy exchange.

I thought when my first wife died my life had come to an end, he would say.

Nothing comes to an end. You never leave anything behind. It always catches up with you.

Perhaps.

No perhaps. It never comes to an end. Not till the end comes.

Friends who dropped in to see them never failed to remark on the wonderful sense of peace emanating from the house high up in the hills above Abergavenny, or to be captivated by his wife's full-throated laugh. As he stuck out his leg and pulled up his trousers to reveal the scar, a hush would descend on the company. But it is not easy to pull a trouser-leg up above the knee and he invariably had to give up his endeavours before he had succeeded, assuring them that the scar was indeed visible after all those years.

It was in Putney, he said, that he had conceived the ambition to translate the sonnets of du Bellay which most appealed to him.

Comme le marinier, que le cruel orage
A long temps agité dessus la haulte mer,
Ayant finablement à force de ramer
Garanty son vaisseau du danger du naufrage,

Regarde sur le port, sans plus craindre la rage
Des vagues ny des vents, les ondes escumer:
Et quelqu'autre bien loing au danger d'abysmer
En vain tendre les mains vers le front du rivage:

Ainsi (mon cher Morel) sur le port arresté
Tu regardes la mer, et vois en seureté,
De mille tourbillons son onde renversee:

Tu la vois jusq'au ciel s'eslever bien souvent,
Et vois ton Du Bellay à la mercy du vent
Assis au gouvernail dans une nef percee.

But ambition is one thing and execution another. Du Bellay's rhymes, so seemingly effortless in French, simply would not transfer into English, no matter how hard he tried. And what of the syntax? We imagine when we start that the subject will be the poet, but it turns out to be his friend Morel, now safe in the harbour, watching the poet, 'at the mercy of the winds, / Sitting at the tiller in a ship full of holes.' It was the combination of quiet precision in the writing and profound despair in what was being written about that never failed to move him. There is his dear Morel on the shore, 'bien loing du danger d'abysmer', well clear of the danger of sinking down into the abyss, gazing out at the ship in trouble in the turbulent seas, and somehow then zooming in on 'your du Bellay', sitting (we are not told what else he is doing, perhaps he is just hopelessly sitting, waiting for the inevitable to happen) at the tiller of the sinking ship. Icy calm and cosmic violence, despair and love and resignation all yoked together in fourteen lines of even rhythm and impeccable rhyme. The wonder of it made him want to cry.

Once, in the library in Putney, as he leafed through a book about nineteenth-century Paris, he noticed a young woman sitting cross-legged on the floor in the next bay, absorbed in a book she had obviously just taken off the shelf. Something about the ease with which she had established herself in this public space and the concentration on her face touched him. He waited to see if she would raise her head from the book but as long as he waited she remained resolutely absorbed in it. He changed his books at the desk and went out, determined to forget all about her, but on the library steps he hesitated, then sat down. He did not know exactly what it was he was waiting for, but he stayed there, looking at the passers-by, dipping into his books, glancing every now and again at his watch. Finally, unable to contain himself any longer, he went back inside and hurried, as though he had forgotten something, to the shelves of travel and geography books. She was still there, exactly as he had left her and still did not look up, even when he stood very close.

He went away again and sat down once more on the low wall outside, but still she did not emerge. Finally, embarrassed by his own actions, he forced himself to leave, walking away quickly without looking back.

After that he went to the library every day, sitting for hours looking through the weekly papers and wandering vaguely from shelf to shelf. But she did not return. At least, not when he was there.

We walk in the labyrinth of our lives, he would say, and we do not know if we are lost or not, do not know if we are happy or not.

Happy, unhappy, his wife – his second wife – would say. It doesn't mean a thing.

That's true too, he would say.

They seemed at such times to be completely unaware of the fact that there were other people there, carrying on a conversation which had no doubt been going on between them for years.

You know me, she would say. I do not hesitate to tell it how it is.

No matter what.

No matter what.

When they went shopping in Abergavenny it was always she who drove and, even in the car, it seemed, their animated conversation never ceased. In the middle of an aisle at the local supermarket they would stop, holding on to the trolley, and talk, making it awkward for the other shoppers to circulate. Friends and neighbours who saw them then would not dare to interrupt, but hurry by with averted eyes and open ears. They never noticed.

It was in his Paris years, he said, that he had come to appreciate the value of silence. The faint hum arising from the rue Saint-Jacques would only make the silence in the room more palpable. I sometimes felt, he would say, that by moving my hand in the air I could alter the pitch of that hum.

He liked to hear the scratching of his pencil as it raced over the paper. I found it soothing, he said. I found it hypnotic. The hours would race by when I was deep in my work and sometimes it was with a start that I realised it was time for my break.

He was a man of regular habits, never carried on past his fixed time of eleven o'clock even when the work was going well. If I had finished in five months instead of six, he would say, what would it have gained me? I would have had to fill up that sixth month with another translation, and it's not as if I had any great belief in the books I was translating or any burning desire to see them out in English sooner than the publisher had planned.

Though translating was my life, he said, I did sometimes wonder why anyone would bother to buy the books on which I worked. There were days, he said, when he could not wait to finish his stint, leave the flat, descend the stairs and then the steps and walk out into the Parisian day.

Sometimes he would take his well-thumbed copy of Shakespeare's poems with him and sit under the shade of the lime trees in the Luxembourg Gardens, reading.

Affection is a coal that must be cooled
Else, suffered, it will set the heart on fire.
The sea hath bounds, but deep desire hath none;
Therefore no marvel though thy hope be gone.

La mer a ses limites mais le désir n'en a. Could he perhaps –

or was that an intolerable arrogance? – turn the whole thing into alexandrines? He would lay the book open on his lap and repeat the words over and over again to himself: *The sea hath bounds but deep desire hath none. The sea hath bounds but deep desire hath none. The sea hath bounds but deep desire hath none.* And: *Heavy heart's lead melt at mine eyes' red fire, / So shall I die by drops of hot desire. Heavy heart's lead melt at mine eyes' red fire. Heavy heart's lead melt at mine eyes' hot fire.* They were words but more than words, rhythm but more than rhythm. If a human being had written those lines, and there was no reason to doubt it, then life was indeed a wonderful thing.

We must never forget, he would say to their guests in the converted farmhouse in the hills above Abergavenny, that Shakespeare is a part of life as much as starving children in Africa and the atrocities of Pol Pot.

Sometimes his wife – his second wife – would ask a few of the guests to stay to lunch. She would rustle up some cold chicken and a salad and they would sit at the old oak table looking out at the valley spread below them. Though people might sometimes have wondered at the precise nature of their relationship, he was eternally grateful to her for having come into his life.

He needed a wife, she would say. I took one look at him and I saw that he needed a wife.

Man is a social animal, he would say, and there comes a time when the strain of having to make every decision for yourself becomes almost unbearable. I had reduced decision-making to a minimum, he would say. I lived my regular life and let the world take care of itself. But there were days when I was afraid to doze off in my chair for fear of never waking up. I felt sometimes that if I let go for a single moment the darkness would invade me and I might never emerge again.

I saved you from the darkness inside you, she would say.

Darkness is a part of each one of us, he would respond.

A part, she would say. When it becomes more than a part it is time to take action.

It was as though I did not want to take up any space in the world, he would say. As though I wanted to be completely invisible.

And yet, he would say, it would not do to exaggerate the negatives. There were moments in his Paris years when he had been happier, he thought, than he had ever been before or since. Moments which he felt to be blessed, he said. Moments when he would thank God, though he did not believe in him, for giving him the life he had. My life and that of no one else, he would say. Realising that it was my life and that of no one else was the most precious gift those Paris years gave me, he said. And so I had to live it as best I could.

To do that you have to forget it is your life, she would say.

That's true too, he would say.

Sometimes you felt he was humouring her, that it was she who was the frail one and it was really he who was in charge. At others you felt the exact opposite. But you always felt that they lived in and for each other and that neither could exist without the other.

Sometimes they drove to the sea and picnicked on the beach. They liked to sit there as night came on, looking out at the infinite expanse of water. You lose yourself when you look at the sea, he would say. The hours go by and you wonder where they went.

Once, on the way back, they passed a burning barn and stopped to look. A fire-engine stood next to it and the firemen, little black figures against the flickering light, were trying to drown the flames in water, to no avail. While they watched the order was given to stand back, and with a strange kind of sigh, as the firemen retreated, the large structure caved in on itself and the conflagration lit up the night sky.

It was that sigh which made the greatest impression on you, she said.

I have never forgotten it, he said. It was as if the entire building had finally resigned itself to its end.

His proudest possession in Paris was his rocking-chair. He had found it in a junk-shop not a mile from where he lived. It was painted a dark green with blue and red flower patterns on the sides, and was upholstered in red silk. As he listened to *Orfeo* he rocked himself gently and felt the music taking him over.

Torn'a l'ombre di morte
Infelice Euridice,
Né più sperar di riveder le stelle,
Ch'omai fia sordo a prieghi tuoi l'Inferno.

Turn again to the shadows of death,
Unhappy Eurydice,
No longer hope to see the stars again,
For henceforth Hades to your prayer is deaf.

It was only in retrospect that he could really savour the complicated play of sounds in 'infelice Euridice … riveder le stelle', for, unlike later opera composers, Monteverdi did not pause and repeat for emphasis but let his music, like life itself, flow on.

Dove t'en vai, mia vita? Ecco, io ti seguo.
Ma chi me 'l niega, oimè? Sogno o vaneggio?

Where are you going, my life? See, I follow you!
But who prevents me, alas? Am I dreaming or delirious?

Sadly, he is neither, and his language and the music both describe and enact his powerlessness in the face of the inevitable.

Qual occulto poter di questi orrori,
Di questi amati orrori,
Mal mio grado mi tragge e mi conduce
A l'odiosa luce?

What occult power among these horrors
Drags me against my will
From these beloved horrors, and leads me
To the loathsome light?

A l'odiosa luce. To the loathsome light. Why did he always shiver with pleasure as he repeated the words to himself? He had known the feeling and it was anything but pleasurable, but there, in Striggio's words and Monteverdi's music, its horror was miraculously transformed, not by being repressed or annihilated but by something much more mysterious to which the phrase 'the power of art' did little justice.

I did not last long as a tutor, he would say. Perhaps it was simply chance that had thrown such difficult students into his path at the very outset, but perhaps too it was something in him that balked at the relationship with his pupils and their families which his role had imposed on all of them, at once servant and tyrant. Swift had railed at it already in the seventeenth century when he accepted the invitation of Sir William Temple and became the tutor of his ward Stella, he said. And nineteenth-century literature was full of accounts of young geniuses forced into the ignominious position of tutoring for a living and being unable to stand it. Often it seemed they took their revenge, if revenge it could be called, by falling in love with the mistress of the house, or, if they were female, the master. But these things did not usually turn out well and, in any case, for good or ill, he had been spared their fate. For after his failure with the Hampstead banker's Marxist daughter he had decided to cut his losses and make do with his poorly paid translation work alone.

You needed your solitude, his wife – his second wife – would say when he talked about these things. You needed your days to yourself.

Yes, he would say, but I could have done with another source of income.

You needed your peace of mind, she would say. It upset you to have to argue with these rich, spoilt young women.

I have to admit I was not much good at tutoring.

You needed your peace of mind.

Sometimes, when he waited, hidden behind the newspaper kiosk, for his wife – his first wife – to come down the steps of Putney Bridge Station, and watched her looking round for him and then starting to walk home on her own, it seemed to him that he did not know her, had merely glimpsed her once or twice before in the High Street or the library or perhaps as he strolled along the towpath. Even when she got out her key and opened the front door of the two-storied Victorian villa in Carlton Drive in which they had their flat, entered and closed the door again behind her, he had the feeling that she was entering a space which was her own and from which he was forever excluded.

He had, he would say, been in a strange state in those first years in Paris after his wife's death. Was he happy? Was he sad? He took each day as it came, kept to his regular routine and endeavoured not to think too much.

Too much thinking can be bad for your health, his wife – his second wife – would say.

Here's to a life without thought, one of the guests would say, and they would all drink to that amidst the laughter.

Sometimes, as he walked through the Parisian streets, he would suddenly be seized with the feeling that he was not there, that all this was still in the future or else in the distant past. He would examine the feeling with detachment, as though it belonged to someone else, and walk on.

Sometimes he and his wife would walk along the towpath as far as Kew Gardens or even Richmond Park. In the trees on the other side of the river at Kew there was a heronry. He remembered passing by there one day in the Spring, he said, and noticing unusual activity in and about the trees. When he stopped to look more attentively he realised that what he was seeing was an endless procession of adult herons bringing food for their young ones hidden in nests in the trees and at once setting off again on the quest for more. Those great noble birds, usually seen standing alone in perfect stillness on the river bank, watching and waiting for their prey, were here flying backwards and forwards like any other birds feeding their young, though the commotion round the nests was a good deal louder and more raucous than that of smaller birds.

He must have stood there for at least half an hour, watching, trying to peer through the foliage to the nests and the young inside them (if you looked carefully you could indeed see both) before finally resuming his walk.

In Paris there was the Ile des Cygnes, Swan Island, but that was an altogether staider affair, in keeping with the formal gardens and general air of symmetry which made parts of the city so elegant and so depressing at the same time.

I saw at once that he was lonely, his wife – his second wife – would say, and I decided then and there to save him from himself.

I was not lonely, I was alone, he would respond. There is a difference.

Not such a big one as all that, she would say.

Besides, he would say, one does not need to be alone to be lonely.

I did not say you did.

True, but you might have been thought to be saying that.

70

He will never cease putting words into my mouth, she would say. While into his I only put good food.

That's true, he would say. With you I have grown fat and contented.

In your mind.

How can one be contented if not in one's mind?

But fat?

Fat too.

Fat too? she would say, incredulous. You think one can be fat in one's mind and thin in one's body?

I do.

Then you are even crazier than I thought.

He had never imagined, when he was living in Paris after the death of his first wife, that he would ever marry again. But life had other ideas.

They all have big plans till my fist comes into contact with their bodies, as the boxer said, she would say.

What boxer?

Some boxer. What does it matter what boxer?

You pride yourself on being the fist life wields?

Yes I do, she would respond. I do pride myself.

There comes a point when you must put everything behind you and start afresh. In his little flat above the Panthéon, he said, he had found a kind of peace.

As he sauntered through Paris on those summer afternoons he sometimes thought: We live in the forests of our dreams and our desires.

The words comforted him. He would go down to the river,

find a quiet spot and open his battered copy of the *Regrets*.

Paschal, je ne veulx point Jupiter assommer,
Ny, comme fit Vulcan, luy rompre la cervelle...

Je ne veulx deguiser ma simple poësie
Sous le masque emprunté d'une fable moisie,
Ny souiller un beau nom de monstres tant hideux:

Mais suivant, comme toy, la veritable histoire,
D'un vers non fabuleux je veulx chanter sa gloire
A nous, à noz enfans, et ceulx qui naistront d'eulx.

Paschal, I have no wish to knock Jupiter out,
Nor, like Vulcan, to split his head in two...

I have no wish to dress up my verse
In the false guise of worn-out myths,
Nor to sully the good name of those monsters of legend.

Instead, like you, I wish to convey the true story,
In simple style to sing her glory,
For us, our children and the children of our children.

That is indeed what he would have liked to do, but when he
tried to render du Bellay's strange and compelling mixture
of formality and directness, let alone to replicate the rhythm
and rhyme that never seemed to be sought but always to be
somehow already there, it proved beyond him. So it would

remain, he felt, for the rest of his life.

Yet the little volume continued both to haunt and to comfort him. He recalled how, having discovered it in the local lending library in Disraeli Road in Putney, he had gone on renewing it month after month until one day the librarian said, as she was about to stamp it for the umpteenth time: Are there no other books you want?

He had not expected to be challenged. He had not expected to be noticed. He gazed at her in alarm. I'm a slow reader in French, he said.

Especially that French, the librarian said, glancing through the book, then stamped it and handed it back to him, looking him full in the face.

He hurried out with it but decided then and there to buy his own copy, though the times were hard and he had to make do with very little. But he didn't like the thought of someone knowing about his private life. Knowing even what books he treasured.

On some Sundays in Paris he would walk across the city to Montmartre and up to the basilica and the tatty, overcrowded Place du Tertre, and then go down the long, straight road leading north to the Porte de Clingancourt and the old flea market there. On other afternoons he would take the metro to the cemetery of Père Lachaise. He liked to track down the tombs of artists he admired, and on one afternoon alone he found those of La Fontaine, Proust, Oscar Wilde, Edith Piaf and the mime Marcel Marceau as well as of Seurat, the great and mysterious disciple of the Impressionists who died so tragically young.

He always had a morbid streak, his wife – his second wife – would say. He was always haunting cemeteries.

Not at all, he would say. I merely wanted to pay homage to the artists I admired.

You can pay homage by reading their books, she would respond. Not by going and sobbing on their graves.

I did not sob, he would say. I gazed.

It's the same thing.

I beg to differ.

Then beg.

They could be seen arguing endlessly in the aisles of the local supermarket, blocking the way to mothers with toddlers and visiting families stocking their holiday homes for the week of their stay.

You do not know what you are talking about, he would be saying to her, and she would be answering, No, it is you who does not know what you are talking about. I beg to differ. Then beg.

He did not remember exactly how it happened. The bank of the river seemed suddenly to give and before he could grab her she was gone. For a moment he thought of jumping in after her but she was a far better swimmer than he, so he ran along the bank beside her, looking for a place where she might be able to climb out.

It was a warm afternoon but she was shivering as she walked beside him, her thin dress sodden and clinging to her. I'll make you a hot grog when we get home, he said. I don't want a hot grog, she said, I want to have a bath and get into some warm clothes. You do that and I'll make you a hot grog for when you get out, he said, but she didn't answer.

It was only after she came out of the bath that she began to cough. She coughed all night and all the next day. He called the doctor, who did not seem unduly worried, prescribed antibiotics and a week off work. But the week went by and the cough did not subside.

In Paris he used to carry Shakespeare's poems around with him and dip into them as he waited for the bus or sipped a coffee in one of his haunts, behind the Odeon or – perhaps his favourite – Le Fumoir in the rue de l'Amiral next to the Louvre.

Had I been toothed like him, I must confess,
With kissing him I should have killed him first.

Or:

No, lady, no; my heart longs not to groan,
But soundly sleeps while now it sleeps alone.

It seemed that, even in an apprentice poem like *Venus and Adonis*, Shakespeare had the words for every feeling and every situation. But why? How does the gift fall upon one man and not upon another?

I was never without that book, he would say. Once I had found it I could not let it go.

His head was always buried in a book, his wife – his second wife – would say. He had difficulty lifting it up to look at the world.

That is an exaggeration, he would say, and you know it.

He would have developed premature curvature of the spine if I had not come along, she would explain.

Another exaggeration, he would say.

He would have ended up completely bent in two.

Listen to her.

I would have had to lie down on the floor to talk to him.

We would have lain down together.

He could not believe his good fortune, he said, the way his life had panned out. Sometimes he felt it was almost too good to be true, and then he imagined a fire ripping through the farmhouse with its many wooden beams, destroying in an instant everything he had. He would stand in the garden watching the firemen struggling with the blaze, the flames rising up into the night sky, and the sound of cracking wood mingling with the acrid smell of smoke and the hiss of the water. He would watch as they carried out her body and hurried it into a waiting ambulance, and then turn to see the high roof finally caving in.

He thought of many things as he walked along the towpath past the famous Harrods Depository and up to Hammersmith Bridge in the hour he allowed himself after lunch, before he returned to the translation that was awaiting him. Sometimes he dropped in to the local fleapit and watched a Truffaut or a Bergman film. There never seemed to be more than half a dozen people there in the afternoon, many of them apparently asleep. He particularly liked coming out again into the open air to find the world exactly as he had left it, as though in his two hours' communion with the silver screen he had, unnoticed, been through more than a normal lifetime's experiences.

In Paris, though there were cinemas all around him, showing every conceivable film from ten in the morning till two the following morning, he found he had lost the desire to go. The thought of sitting in a darkened auditorium and watching a drama which had nothing to do with him unfold on the flickering screen had grown repulsive. Music, not moving images, was what he now craved.

Qual occulto poter di questi orrori,
Da questi amati orrori
Mal mio grado mi tragge e mi condusce
A l'odiosa luce?

What occult power among these horrors,
drags me against my will
from these horrors I love and leads me
to the loathsome light?

A l'odiosa luce. He knew what that meant, to want to live in darkness forever, never to have to get up, never to have to draw the curtains and see the light of day. *L'odiosa luce.*

He had always felt that the final act of *Orfeo* was a collective failure of nerve. Orpheus is drawn up into heaven by Apollo, the two of them singing for all they are worth.

Saliam cantando al Cielo
Dove ha virtù verace
Degno premio di sé, diletto e pace.

Let us singing rise to Heaven
where true virtue
has its due reward – joy and peace.

Is that not an insult to all that has preceded it? he asked. The court of Mantua may have wanted this, he said, but no one listening to the opera today could possibly accept it. *Orfeo*, he said, dealt with the death of social and heavenly harmony and with the birth of the solo voice, lamenting its own emergence and the end of millennia of choric chant. It heralds the public acknowledgement of the demise of plainsong and all it had stood for, he said, the community of Christian souls affirming their common faith through communal chanting, and of the birth of the individual, isolated, lost, inconsolable, yet able in despair to sing in a way that had never been heard before and that brought tears to the eyes of the listeners and made them feel they were in touch with their deepest selves. Such song, he said, heralds the birth of *bel canto* and of the dying diva's lament. In Orpheus, he said, the soulful crooner finds his voice and after him the pop star.

Though few could follow him when he took off like this they would listen to him in rapt attention, enjoying his erudition and his passion. Afterwards a few friends would stay to a simple lunch, the local doctor and his highborn Indian wife, a retired civil servant and his horse-faced wife, an Oxford classicist who refused ever to talk about his work and who, when asked what his field was, would reply that fields were for donkeys.

Once, when the only guests were the civil servant and his wife, she cornered him between the sofa and the bookcase.

Look at them! she hissed. It's disgusting!

What is? he asked.

The way they carry on.

I'm sorry?

Anyone can see what's going on.

I'm afraid I don't follow you, he said.

You know, she said, looking him full in the face, that's exactly what it is: you are afraid.

He tried to move away but she followed and pinned him to the bookcase.

Do something about it! she hissed. You understand?

Please, he said.

Because if you don't I will.

Standing in the frozen garden he watched the flames rise into the night sky and listened to the roar of the fire as it devoured the wooden beams, mingled with the hiss of the ineffectual jets of water the firemen were still pumping into the rapidly disintegrating building.

We thought that was the end of our dream, his wife – his second wife – would say. But it's amazing how much of the damage proved to be superficial.

I'm a survivor, she would say. Nobody can deny that I'm a survivor. You wouldn't believe the number of times in my life that everything seemed at an end and yet I always pulled through.

You always pull through, he would echo.

He knows me well, she would say. I always do.

Yes. You always do.

Sometimes he would walk across the Luxembourg Gardens to the Montparnasse cemetery where Baudelaire is buried, and sit there on a bench among the tombstones, thinking of nothing.

I seem to have passed my life finding places where I could sit and simply think of nothing, he would say. In Putney there was a bench on the towpath where the river curves between Hammersmith Bridge and Barnes. In Paris, the cemetery of Montparnasse in particular. Besides Baudelaire, Sartre and Simone de Beauvoir are buried there, in the same tomb, as well as Robert Desnos, the marvellous poet murdered by the Nazis, and many of those foreign artists who made Paris their home in the first part of the twentieth century: Tristan Tzara, his fellow Romanian Constantin Brâncuşi, Soutine, Zadkine, the South Americans César Vallejo and Julio Cortázar, and many others, including André Citroën, the manufacturer of France's best-loved car. Unlike the Père Lachaise cemetery in the northeast of the city, with its weird baroque monuments, and unlike the largely treeless cemetery of Montmartre in the north, this cemetery in the south exudes a sense of peace and serenity. He would not bother to take a book with him when he set off there, he said, because he knew what he would do when he arrived: find his favourite bench, sit staring out into space, and let his mind go blank.

He sometimes talked about his early days in Putney in the south west of London. Putney, in those days, he would say, still had the feeling of post-war austerity. At the corner of the High Street and the Upper Richmond Road, and next to the Rotary Club, stood the Kardomah Café, which served the warm and watery brew that in those days passed for coffee in Britain. It always seemed to be empty and one could sit by the window and gaze out at the drab and busy High Street which had once been a portion of the road that led from London to Portsmouth and which still had a surprising number of double-decker buses trundling up and down from the Heath to the Bridge and, from there, by diverse routes, to central London and all points north and east.

One day, seeing a young woman seated at another window, he ventured to go up to her and ask if he could sit down.

She looked up, surprised. Do I know you? she asked.

I don't think so, he said.

She made a gesture towards the rest of the room. There are lots of empty tables, she said.

He stood there, feeling foolish but determined not to back off.

She motioned him to a chair. Sit down, she said.

I haven't seen you here before, he said.

I haven't seen you.

True, he conceded.

She waited, looking out of the window.

I come here a great deal, he said. I like the fact that it's so empty.

She had pale blonde hair and a dimple in her right cheek. She turned to face him. Why aren't you working? she asked.

I work at home.

He waited for her to ask him what he did but she was silent, so he ventured the information himself: I translate, he said.

She looked at him. He bent over his coffee.

Since she said nothing he looked up and asked: Do you live here?

Uh-huh.

And what do you do?

This and that.

Meaning?

Oh...

Do you walk? he asked her.

Walk?

I mean do you like walking?

Uh-huh.

Do you ever walk to Kew?

I've done it, she said.

Would you like to do it with me?

She shrugged her shoulders.

What about the day after tomorrow?

All right.

They had agreed to meet at two in front of the church by the bridge. Having initiated it, however, he found himself wondering why he had done so. And when the time came he found himself sitting at the back of a café in the High Street with a view of the church. From there he watched her arrive, stand there, look at her watch, look around her, walk to the corner of the church and back, look round once more, look again at her watch, and walk away.

A few days later he caught sight of her in the High Street. He quickened his step to catch up with her, then slowed again and followed her as she turned down Lacy Road. Here the crowds thinned and he held back, afraid she would turn round and see him. But she seemed lost in her own thoughts and uninterested in anything around her. She turned again down a side street and he was afraid he had lost her. He quickened his pace and when he reached a corner there she was, some sixty feet ahead of him. He slowed again and let her gain a little distance, for now they were the only two people in the quiet suburban street, but he need not have worried, for she had climbed the stairs to the door of one of the small Victorian terraced houses that lined the street and was inserting a key into the lock of a blue door. From a distance he watched the door open and then close again. He became aware of the silence lying upon the street.

Now that he knew where she lived he found himself, most days, walking past her door on the way down to the river. He never saw her. One day, though, when his mind was elsewhere, he caught sight of her on the towpath ahead of him, walking in the direction of Hammersmith Bridge. He fell into step behind her and so they proceeded. As they were passing the Harrods Depository she suddenly stopped and turned. He too stopped, not more than twenty feet away from her, and they looked at each other. Holding his gaze, she very slowly shook her head. He turned quickly then and started to hurry back in the direction he had come. And though he occasionally caught sight of her again in the street and shops of Putney he never again tried to follow or speak to her.

He lived his life in a dream, his wife – his second wife – would say. He did not have a firm grasp of reality.

Every young man is allowed to dream, he would respond.

Only if he can wake up.

You don't think I woke up?

Not till half your life was over.

Half my life?

At least.

Perhaps.

Perhaps, perhaps, she would say, mocking him. All he can say is perhaps.

The first time he visited the *marché des puces* at the Porte de Clignancourt he bought a silver soup-ladle. He had no need of a soup-ladle since he never cooked for himself, but this particular spoon had taken his fancy and for the first time in his life he found himself bargaining with the storekeeper, something he had never felt the least inclination to do, perhaps because he sensed that he would not be very good at it, that he lacked conviction in such situations. But something drove him that day when the man named his price to offer him a tenth of what he asked. The man laughed, then to his surprise offered him the spoon for half the price he had initially mentioned. Eventually they agreed on a sum just short of half that and the man wrapped up the spoon in tissue paper, seemingly greatly satisfied, and they shook hands on it. Back in the flat he put it on a shelf where he would sometimes take it down to polish it and was always pleased to see it.

Everything he did he did *assiduously*, his wife – his second wife – would say. He has always done everything *assiduously*.

It was the combination of surprising detail and general reflection he found so satisfying in du Bellay, as in the opening of the fifty-sixth sonnet of the *Regrets*.

Baïf, qui, comme moy, prouves l'adversité,
Il n'est pas tousjours bon de combatre l'orage,
Il faut caler la voile, et de peur du naufrage,
Ceder à la fureur de Neptune irrité.

Baïf, he who (like me) has experienced adversity,
Knows it's rarely wise to fight against the storm:
Better lower the sail and, for fear of shipwreck,
Give way to the fury of an angry sea.

'It's rarely wise' fails of course to capture the delightful under-statement of 'il n'est tousjours bon', but 'it's not always wise' seemed too plonking to him. As for 'angry sea', it certainly did not do justice to 'Neptune irrité', but 'angry Neptune' was hardly an option. And so it went. It seemed to him that, what-ever mood he was in, there would be a poem in the *Regrets* to reflect it. He loved the solid, almost stolid building blocks of these poems, their foursquare occupation of the space, their total lack of sentimentality or whimsy. My life felt so insubstan-tial at the time, he would say, it was a blessing to find these stur-dy, no-nonsense poems, which nevertheless resonated with a mysterious power. I clung to them as a drowning man to a raft.

Mysterious power, she would mock. Mysterious power. He was always looking for saviours in his life.

That's true, he would say. Perhaps I have that propensity.

When I first met him, she would say, I hardly understood what he was saying, he used so many funny words.

I told you, he would say. I told you I was an old-fashioned person.

85

He never went out without his hat.

Yes, always with my hat.

Summer or winter, always with his hat.

I felt naked without it.

You wished to insulate yourself against the world.

Perhaps I did.

Perhaps, she would say. He thinks that by saying perhaps he can protect himself against reality.

We all try to protect ourselves against reality.

But some more than others.

Some more than others, he admitted.

Friends who had known him in the old days were amazed at his new-found calm, at the way he would accept criticism of himself and shrug it off, and they attributed it all to his wife and to the sense of calm and peace that seemed to follow wherever she went.

Sometimes, when he met his wife – his first wife – at the Putney Bridge underground station, they would not cross the footbridge but turn instead towards Putney Bridge and take the passage under the road to reach the riverside gardens which led past the old palace of the Bishops of London and on to Craven Cottage, the Fulham football ground, and so via a maze of small empty streets behind the river to Hammersmith Bridge and then back along the south bank of the river, where the towpath was continuous. If the weather was particularly fine they would go into the garden of the Bishop's Palace, with its walled inner garden and, hidden from the general view, one of the most magical trees he had ever seen, a sixty-yard wisteria that enclosed what had once been a vibrant kitchen and herb garden, though now it consisted only of a sorry array of overgrown lots and broken greenhouses through which the weeds grew, unchecked.

When the wisteria was in flower, he said, and it flowered twice a year, its strange unearthly beauty, more grey than blue, but a vibrant grey, if that can be imagined, a subtle, ever-changing grey, always made him want to cry, though whether for joy or sorrow he could not tell. They would take their fill of it and then lie on the grass beyond, under the neglected apple trees, and look up at the bright blue sky through the orange and white blossom or the little hard red apples just visible through the leaves.

There is a kind of sorrow in solitude, he would say. The sweetness and the sadness are conjoined. And Monteverdi is the artist of that mood. It is, he would say, the mood of our times, for however close we are to another human being we always know, deep down, that we are alone.

They could often be seen driving out on excursions to the Brecon Beacons or even to the beaches of South Wales, she at the wheel and he, animated as ever, in the seat beside her.

He talks and I listen, she would say. Every relationship, if it is successful, has to have in it one person who talks and one who listens.

Don't I listen? he would ask.

Not always.

That's true, he would concede.

He liked to stand at the large plate-glass window and look out across the valley while she busied herself in the kitchen. She knew the dishes he liked and what it was that agreed and did not agree with his delicate stomach. I look after him all right, she would say.

You do.

You see? she would say. For once he agrees with me.

I invariably agree with you.

It's his use of words like that, she would say, that first drew me to him. I had never met anyone who used so many long words.

They seem natural to me.

That's what I mean, she would say.

Sometimes, as he made his way to Putney Bridge Station to wait for her to arrive, he did not know whether he would come forward to greet her when she appeared or conceal himself behind the newspaper kiosk. And he did not know either why he concealed himself when he did and then followed her as if she was a stranger until she walked up the steps of the Victorian villa in which they had their flat, searched in her bag, produced the keys, fitted one into the lock, opened the door and then closed it again behind her, without a backward glance, as if shutting him out of her life forever:

Torn'a l'ombre di morte,
Infelice Euridice,
Né piu sperar di riveder le stele,
Ch' omai fia sordo a prieghi tuoi l'Inferno.

Return to the shadows of death,
Unhappy Eurydice,
And hope no more to see the stars again,
For henceforth Hades is deaf to your prayers.

The speed with which she sank was the thing that most surprised him. He had expected her to splash out, to try and swim, even if, for some reason, it proved difficult. But there was only the splash and then nothing. He stared at the water in bafflement, waiting for her to surface, but there was nothing. It was as if some force was there, deep in the river, waiting to drag her down.

What did you do then? they asked at the police station when he reported it.

I sat down, he said.

You sat down?

Yes.

What do you mean, you sat down?

I sat down and waited for her to reappear.

You didn't think of jumping in after her?

No, he said.

Why not?

I don't know.

Try to remember, they said.

I told you, he said after a while. I thought she would re-appear.

But when she didn't?

I didn't know where she was.

What do you mean you didn't know where she was?

I didn't know where to jump in. She might have swum under water. Or the current might have carried her.

So what did you do?

I came here.

He waited.

Have you sent a team to find her? he asked after a while.

Yes, they said.

She may have got her leg caught in something.

But then why didn't you jump in?

I don't know.

Do you want to call a lawyer? they asked him.

What for? he said.

To advise you.

I don't need anyone to advise me, he said. I need to get her out.

Unbelievable, his wife – his second wife – would say, when he recounted this in the large living room of their converted farmhouse in the Black Mountains above Abergavenny. To lose your wife and then be treated as a suspect by the police. Unbelievable.

They were only doing their duty.

Their first duty was to try and save her.

That is what happens in such cases, he would say. I understood their point of view.

You were in shock, she would say. Or you would never have answered their questions.

Sometimes, after lunch, his wife – his second wife – would put a jazz record on the gramophone and then she and Wilfred would dance while he and Mabel looked on, or he gazed out of the window at the glorious view spread out before him. Come on, Mabel, Wilfred would say, have a go, both of you. I am not the dancing type, she would respond, while he pretended not to hear.

What he liked about du Bellay's *Regrets* was that the poems were not addressed to a single mistress, as were those of so many of his contemporaries, infatuated more by Petrarch than by any individual woman, but to the many real friends he had left behind in France when, in 1553, he was ordered to follow his cousin, the cardinal Jean du Bellay, to Rome. And yet these poems – and there is no hint of any homosexual liaison – are as passionate and intense as any by Scève or Ronsard – more so for sounding so natural and unforced. Take sonnet forty-one, he would say.

> N'estant de mes ennuis la fortune assouvie,
> A fin que je devinsse à moy-mesme odieux,
> M'osta de mes amis celuy que j'aymois mieux,
> Et sans qui je n'avois de vivre nulle envie.

> Donc l'eternelle nuict a ta clarté ravie,
> Et je ne t'ay suivy parmy ces obscurs lieux?
> Toy, qui m'as plus aymé que ta vie et tes yeux,
> Toy, que j'ay plus aymé que mes yeux et may vie.

The rather conventional first stanza suddenly gives way to something utterly different, a tragedy and a lament which would not be out of place in *Orfeo*.

> Not satisfied with the blows she had dealt me,
> And determined to render me hateful to myself,
> Fortune took away the friend I loved the most,
> Making me lose the very will to live.

Thus eternal night has robbed you of the light,
Yet I failed to follow you to those dark regions?
You who loved me more than your life and your eyes,
You, whom I loved more than my eyes and my life.

You ask, he would say, where is the rhyme and where is the rhythm, the English equivalent of the subtle French alexandrine? And I have to confess that it is not there. I had by then long given up trying to translate poetry into poetry. For my own sake I found rough English equivalents, but what could I do, in twentieth-century English, with the weight of *moymesme*, of *aymois,* of *nuict* and *parmy,* not to speak of the unforced rhymes of *assouvie, envie, ravie* and *vie,* or *odieux, mieux, lieux* and *yeux*? Rather than rail against the poverty of my vocabulary and powers of invention, rather than spend sleepless nights turning over a quatrain until I could hear the rumble of the city beginning to come to life, I preferred simply to read these poems and even learn them by heart.

But it's true, he would say, that some of the excitement went out of my reading when I gave up my self-imposed task, and I felt as well that, however hard I read them, I did not enter their very being in the way I felt I had when I was actively engaged in the task of translation.

Though they searched the smouldering ruins the police found no clue as to the cause of the conflagration. There was no reason to consider arson, though some holiday homes had been targeted by Welsh nationalists in the past. But those tended to belong to people who used them only occasionally, whereas they had been living in the converted farmhouse ever since they had bought it. Did anyone have a grudge against them? they were asked, but they could think of no one. On the contrary, not only were they popular with their friends, they were well liked in the town, where they were always ready to banter with the butcher or commiserate with the supermarket checkout girls. Friends and acquaintances would stop them in the street for a chat or stand looking on with a smile as they took up the middle of the pavement, engaged in animated discussion and oblivious of what was going on around them.

He was a man of regular habits. Once he had found a restaurant to his taste he stayed faithful to it. He was happy to eat whatever was put in front of him but he was always pleased when there was vegetable soup to begin with and *crème caramel* to end. Though he was not averse to meat he had asked to be spared the tripe and brains that were sometimes on offer, and he particularly enjoyed the fish that was regularly served on Fridays. He abhorred milk in his coffee and rarely drank more than a single glass of white wine with his meal.

His stomach was his Achilles heel, his wife – his second wife – would interrupt.

I like to feel well, he would respond. That is more important to me than eating even the most succulent repast.

You do. And I make sure you always do, she would say.

As he sat on his favourite bench in the Cimetière de Montparnasse he often recalled the day when he and his wife – his first wife – had first stumbled upon the mysterious lost and overgrown cemetery on Putney Heath, on the way to Barnes. Unlike the well-laid-out cemeteries of Paris and indeed of France as a whole, neatly walled and with all the tombstones set in orderly rows, this one seemed to have no clear boundaries and the tombstones appeared to grow like the trees in whose midst they appeared, randomly and without logic. Many of the statues had been vandalised over the ages and there were a great many decapitated angels. Originally perhaps there had been some attempt at order and symmetry, for somewhere near the centre a space had been cleared and a memorial to a certain William Hedgeman, in the form of a large cross standing on an inscribed plinth, had been erected. But three of the four paths leading to it from the sides had lost all semblance of straightness, the way been blocked by fallen trees and more gravestones, overgrown now by creepers and moss. Many of those buried in this mysterious place appeared to be Dutch, according to the names and the inscriptions on the gravestones, though why he had no idea, and no one seemed to have been buried there after 1940. He was pleased though to find the grave of Francis Palgrave (1824–1897), the editor of the much-loved Victorian poetry anthology *Palgrave's Golden Treasury*, resident of Twickenham and one-time Professor of Poetry at Oxford, as well as that of Ebenezer Cobb Morley (1831–1924), regarded, said the inscription, as the father of modern football, and of Julia Martha Thomas (d. 1879), described simply and suggestively as 'murder victim'. She was in fact, he discovered in the local library, the victim of one of the most famous murders of the Victorian era, killed in a fight with her Irish servant, who then cut off her head and sliced up her body, boiling the dismembered parts before burying some of them and throwing the rest in the river. For some reason, perhaps in order to sell the furniture, she impersonated her mistress for several weeks before being rumbled and fleeing to Ireland where the police found her and brought her back to England to stand trial at the Old Bayley. The head of her victim, though, was not found until 1952, when workmen enlarging the house of the naturalist David Attenborough unearthed it. How many other secrets lie buried under our cities, parks and heaths, he wondered?

A road went through Putney Heath just beyond the cemetery and what seemed to be municipal tennis courts had at some point been laid close to it. As one crept through the trees, parting the undergrowth to see what lay beneath, one could hear the smack of ball against racket and the cheerful shouts of the players. That was the world of the living.

They had been walking across the Heath one Saturday morning on their way to the pub in Barnes where, on weekends, they occasionally liked to eat, when they had come across the cemetery. They must have passed within yards of it on numerous previous occasions without stumbling upon it, and even after many visits there was always the sense of suddenly and unexpectedly entering a lost world.

You see? his wife – his second wife – would say when he came to this point in his story. At heart he is a romantic.

Perhaps I am, he would say.

Perhaps, she would mock him. Perhaps. It is his favourite word.

What would we do without it?

We would live our lives more happily, she would respond.

More happily perhaps, he would come back at her, but more humanly? More richly?

Who is he to talk to me about the richness of life? she would say. I ask you. The richness of life is living in the present with what you have.

He would put his foot on the arm of the sofa and draw up the leg of his trousers to show them the scar. It's still there, he would say. After all these years.

And why is it still there? she would ask. It is there because you want it to be there.

What I want doesn't come into it, he would say. It is there because it will not go away.

And why will it not go away?

Who knows? he would say.

Who knows? Who knows? she would mock. I'll tell you who knows. I know.

He could not believe that the charred bodies he was shown had once been living people. He could not recognise the other corpse they had dragged from the burning house. On his way out he saw Mabel, but she pretended not to see him and he for his part had nothing to say to her.

A long night, he thought.

It was as he sat under a tree in the Old Barnes Cemetery, as he discovered it was called, that the idea of moving to Paris first came to him. At first he simply toyed with it as one of those fantasies it's fun to have but which are so far beyond the bounds of possibility that they can safely be indulged. The cost of travel to such worlds is minimal, as is the effort required. There are no plans to make, no suitcases to pack, no precious possessions to dispose of. You sit under a tree, on an over-grown tombstone perhaps, and you are there, or there, or there.

But as is the way with the imagination, thinking frequently and long enough about something makes it seem at first possible, then even probable, and, finally, necessary. And that is how he got to Paris, he would say. First by imagining, then by asking himself why not, and finally he was there, rocking himself in the rocker in his little flat high up above the streets of Paris, listening to the strains of *Orfeo* on the gramophone or sitting on his favourite bench beneath the trees in the cemetery of Montparnasse, his eyes open but unseeing, or walking along the river looking at the city reflected in its placid waters, or up the hill and over the Butte de Montmartre on his way to the flea market at the Porte de Clignancourt.

As he walked he thought of the way she had bent to put the key in the lock, then straightened and entered, closing the door behind her. And he thought too of the way their eyes had locked that day on the towpath and she had looked at him and slowly shaken her head.

As soon as I saw him I knew he needed to get married, his wife – his second wife – would say. He had been alone long enough.

I did not need to get married, he would say. I chose to do so.

You can call it instinct, she would say. But as soon as I saw him I knew it.

Instinct she has in abundance, he would say.

He needed someone to take care of him, she would say.

I was perfectly capable of taking care of myself, he would respond. I had after all done so for many years.

You had done so because you had to, she would say. It was not what you chose.

How do people know what they have chosen and not chosen? he would ask. They may think they have not chosen but perhaps in reality they have.

Listen to him, she would say. He never sticks to the subject but always manages to generalise. It's another way of avoiding life.

Perhaps, he would say.

I may not be well educated, she would say, but one thing is for sure, I never avoided life.

That's true, he would say.

Their banter, which in other couples might have been a way of fighting private battles in public, was with them always loving and always half ironic. It was also deeply ritualistic. You felt it was their way of expressing pride in each other.

As she stood in the middle of the room, carefully wiping a record before reverentially handing it to him, he would gaze at her in love and admiration. He lowered the needle and they heard the orchestra strike up. Orpheus sang:

Fu ben felice il giorno,
Mio ben, che pria ti vidi,
E più felice l'ora
Che per te sospirai,
Poich' al mio sospirar tu sospirasti;
Felicissimo il punto
Che la candida mano,
Pegno di pura fede, a me porgesti.

Happy was the day,
O my treasure, when first I saw you,
And happier still the hour
When first for you I sighed,
For you too at my sighing sighed;
But happiest of all the moment
When you gave me your snow-white hand,
A pledge of faith eternal.

By staging this drama of loss, he said, Monteverdi discovers depths of feeling and expression in both music and the voice that no one before him had known existed. But there is no hiding that it is, nonetheless, a loss.

In Putney he had spent many afternoons in the local flea-pit in the Chelverton Road, just off the High Street. I do not know if it still exists today, he would say; even in those days I was at times the only person there, watching some Fellini or Bergman film, totally absorbed. And it gave me a particular pleasure to come out into the sunlight, he would say, and walk slowly through the backstreets down to the river. There I would lean over the railings and gaze down into the water.

Minutes, sometimes hours would go by. When he finally looked up and stepped back the sky was already darkening and he knew it was time to go home. Slowly he would retrace his steps, perhaps stopping on the way to buy something for supper.

In Paris, he thought, he would forge himself a new life, free of the melancholy that seemed to hang over Putney, whatever the weather, the pervasive feeling that nothing had ever happened there and nothing ever would, free of the perpetual greyness which seemed to cling to the place even on bright summer days.

He wondered if other people felt this. His best friend at Oxford had been fond of quoting the remark that 'the world of the happy man is other than the world of the unhappy man'. Perhaps, he thought, this was the world he carried with him and would go on carrying no matter where he lived. Nevertheless, the idea of Paris continued to haunt him, its streets and cafés, its old houses, its gardens and squares, its cathedral and its river. He liked to stroll along the *quais*, stopping to browse in the little bookstalls set up against the wall, occasionally picking up a copy of the poems of Nerval or the essays of Georges Bataille. It was there he had come across the *Regrets* of du Bellay, and the title had immediately struck a chord in him. There was so much to regret, so much that could have been different.

The opening words enchanted him. The volume begins with a dedicatory poem to a Monsieur d'Avanson, who was, according to the notes, 'Counsellor to the King in his Private Council'. But instead of the expected effusions there is only a series of bleak quatrains, the first of which sets the tone for the whole volume.

Si je n'ay plus la faveur de la Muse,
Et si mes vers se trouvent imparfaits,
Le lieu, le temps, l'aage ou je les ay faits,
Et mes ennuis leur serviront d'excuse.

If I'm no longer in the good books of the Muse,
And if my verses seem ill-formed,
The place, the time, my youth, my genes, my woes –
All these can serve as my excuse.

But there is, of course, no excuse. For it is not really his art but his life that he is talking about, and for one's life not living up to expectation there is no excuse, except for the paltry one that this is true of everybody's life.

He would talk of his fantasies of drowning, vivid images he experienced when he was living in Paris, after the death of his first wife. As I sank I would feel quite relieved, he would say. I would think: There goes another life – and know I had not finished with this one.

One sprouts so many lives, he would say, and look at her and smile. One is a murderer. One an incendiary. One a suicide. One lives in London. One in Paris. One in New York.

One, one, one, she would echo, mocking him.

With his grey hat pulled low over his eyes he climbs the stairs out of the rue Saint Julien.